UNION
COUNTY

by

KEN FARMER

Cover Art by:
Ken Farmer
Adriana Girolami

ISBN-13: 978-1-7363220-2-4
Timber Creek Press
Imprint of Timber Creek Productions, LLC
312 N. Commerce St.
Gainesville, Texas 76240

Published by: Timber Creek Press
timbercreekpresss@yahoo.com
www.timbercreekpress.net
Twitter: @pagact
Facebook Book Page:
www.facebook.com/TimberCreekPress
Ken's email: pagact@yahoo.com
214-533-4964

DEDICATION

This tome is dedicated to my mother and father, Robert R. 'Joe' Farmer - 1908 to 1965, and Johnie Vertis Jolley Farmer - 1915 to 1974.

ACKNOWLEDGMENT

The author gratefully acknowledges Lt. Colonel Clyde DeLoach, USMC (Ret.), T.C. Miller, Terry Heflin - retired English Professor at Tarrant County College, best-selling author, Brad Dennison, and Cynthia Morast-Foster, teacher, for their invaluable help in proofing, beta reading and editing this novel.

TIMBER CREEK PRESS

CHAPTER ONE

JAMISON HOME

"Hutch is what?"

I stared at grandpa while I warmed my hiney in front of the fireplace. Tiny was curled up on the rag rug next to me, warmin' herself, too.

He leaned forward in his rocker an' spat a long yellow stream of snuff juice into the fire. It splattered on a burnin' log an' sizzled for a minute before steamin' away. Me an' Tiny made sure we were on the side of the big wide fireplace so grandpa had plenty of room to spit in the fire.

"The sheriff has him in for questioning on some burglaries in the area...and a murder. An older widow woman...near eighty."

I was gobsmacked, that was a word I'd heard at school. We'd just got there from Fort Morgan, Colorado, where daddy had been transferred from Junction City, Arkansas, a couple months ago.

It was two weeks before Christmas an' daddy decided to take his vacation at Shell Oil to come to southern Arkansas in the winter to get away from the snow an' ice in Colorado where they'd been drillin' for oil—didn't work.

It was cold as the dickens when we got here, with snow expected—yea.

'Course, this bein' southern Arkansas, the snow, ice, an' cold doesn't usually last too long. It's liable to be sixty degrees in two or three days—keeps it interestin' that way.

Mister Tom had moved into the cabin down in the woods near the pond with Unka Dud as he was still recouperatin' from the gunshot wound he got when we tangled with those Germans last summer.

We had all been tasked by Unka Dud to help take care of the secret treasure he'd been guardin' for thirty-five years.

"There ain't no way Hutch ever robbed anybody...much less killin', Grandpa. No way!"

He nodded. "I know, I know, Foot. We all are aware Hutch wouldn't do something like this." He spat again an' wiped the dribble from his chin. "But someone said they saw him at old Miz Riggs house...the lady that got killed."

"At it or near it?"

"That's a good point, Foot. We'll have to find out...There have been a number of burglaries around here, but apparently, this time, the owner, in this case, the widow Riggs, walked in on 'em. Her daughter, who lives 'bout a half mile away, found her...She'd been beaten to death."

Mama put her hand over her mouth. "My God."

"Grandpa, ain't no way a ten year old boy like me or Hutch could beat somebody to death...Uh-uh, no way, no day."

Daddy sat down in another rocker in front of the fireplace. The fireplaces—there were three but weren't hardly ever lit at the same time—were the only sources of heat in the house, 'cept for grandma's cookstove in the kitchen, 'cause they still didn't have electricity or gas. The co-op had promised—but still nothin'.

Grandpa was thinkin' 'bout gettin' one of those big propane tanks for a new stove for grandma, but she said she likes her wood burnin' cookstove.

"What's the thief stealin', John?"

Grandpa still carried a deputy sheriff's badge an' was called for help from time to time by Sheriff Wilson.

"I investigated several of the robberies myself, Joe, an' the usual stuff...cash, jewelry, guns, and the like. They always pick old folks...I believe they watch the house and the mail delivery then pick the week after they know the owner gets a check an' has the time to go to town to the bank and cash it."

"Sounds a little sophisticated for a ten year old, doesn't it?"

"I'd say."

Grandma came in the parlor. "Vertis, come help me bring the coffee and cocoa in."

"All right, Mama."

My mom got up an' followed grandma down the wide dog run to the kitchen.

"How many witnesses saw Hutch?"

Grandpa looked from daddy to me. "One."

My mouth fell open. "One?...And how did they describe him?"

"Colored boy, nine or ten, short nappy hair..."

Daddy rolled his eyes.

SHERIFF'S OFFICE, UNION COUNTY

"What were you doing over there on Sweet Road, last Sunday afternoon, Hutch? That's a couple of miles from your grandparents house, idn't it?"

Sheriff Wilson leaned back in his wood swivel chair, clasped his fingers over his round belly and studied Hutch while he waited for an answer.

"One of the Collins boys told me at school he'd seen some pawpaws over down near the branch...Even ate one when they were almost ripe earlier...Got sick as a dog. I was goin' to get grandma some of those big dry pawpaw leaves she wanted for one of her poultices...That's all...Honest Injun, Sheriff."

"You didn't stop at Miz Riggs place?"

Hutch frowned. "Miz Riggs? No, Sir...no way. She don't like us coloreds. I walk on the other side of the road whenever I got to go by her place."

"You ever talk to her?"

Hutch shook his head. "Uh-uh. Ain't crazy...she's mean. Give you what for with that hickory cane of hers."

Sheriff Wilson stifled a grin. "See anybody drive by when you were walking on that road?"

Hutch turned his head and thought for a moment. "Old man Green, in that Plymouth pickup truck of his. He just glares atcha when he drives past...Don't think he likes coloreds much either."

"See him before or after you passed Miz Riggs place?"

"Ah...before. By 'bout a quarter-mile."

"Anybody else?"

"Uh...saw a couple fellas go by when I was at the branch pickin' up leaves. The pawpaw trees is right near fifty yards down the branch from the road."

"Tell who it was?"

"Nawsir, they's stirrin' up too much dust...could just tell there was two of 'em."

"What kind of truck?"

"Not sure on that neither...but it was a blue one, though."

"New or old?"

"Well, wadn't old as old man Green's. Think his was made 'fore the war."

"Yeah...Those two see you?"

Hutch shook his head. "Uh-uh. Hard to tell...in the dust an' all."

"Where'd you get that silver dollar you had in your pocket?"

"Mister John. He gave me an' Foot each one. Look on the date an' you'll see it was made the year he was borned...1883."

"You don't say?"

"Yessir, just did."

The sheriff frowned, picked up the Morgan silver dollar that was on his desk along with a sling shot and a red and white yo-yo and looked at the date through his bifocals.

"Huh, sure does...Don't lose this, Hutch, might be worth some money one day...more than just a dollar."

"Really?"

He nodded. "Could be."

"Can I go home now? Got a letter from Foot that said they were drivin' down from Colorado...Be here sometime today."

"I'll just take you to John's. How's that."

"Close enough...'Preciate it, Sheriff."

"You stay where I can find you, all right?"

Hutch nodded. "Yessir."

"Get your stuff there." The sheriff pointed to the things from Hutch's pockets on his desk.

He grabbed the items and put them back where he normally carried them, and then got his coat from the back of the chair and put it on.

"All right, get your coat back on and let's go."

Sheriff Wilson picked his jacket and gray Stetson from the tree, set the hat on his head, and slipped the military style fleece-lined leather jacket on as they exited the door to his office.

JAMISON HOME

I saw the sheriff pull his black Ford up next to the white Chevrolet Stanley Coffee van parked out in front of grandpa's house.

The company had a bunch of sales routes in southern Arkansas serving folks who lived too far from town to just run into the store like we do in town. Most of 'em visited the houses like grandma an' grandpa's on a regular basis every two weeks or so with coffee, lard, flour, sugar, tobacco, and stuff like needles and thread.

I was beside grandma who was talkin' to the salesman standing on the stoop. He was holding his order pad writin' down what grandma wanted.

We looked out at the sheriff as he and Hutch got out of his car.

"Ya'll get out, Myron. Glad you brought Hutch back. Come on in and get yourself warm by the fire in the parlor while Clyde here gets my order and the stuff Tom Rayford wanted."

I jumped down off the porch an' ran out to the gate as they came in. "Hey, Hutch!"

"Hey, Foot!"

We hugged like men do with a lots of backpoundin', then standin' back an' tradin' punches to the shoulder—hadn't seen one another since we moved to Colorado from Junction City last September. It was only 'bout two weeks after our little set to with them Germans when my cousin Fran was here from Texas that daddy got transferred.

"You didn't get arrested?"

He looked up at Sheriff Wilson, then at me. "Uh-uh."

"I was just talking to him, Foot."

I nodded. "Oh, like what they call interrogatin' in the movies."

He grinned. "Well, something like that. I just call it gettin' information."

"In the movies they always wind up puttin' 'em in jail."

Hutch whacked me again, only harder this time. "Whose side are you on, anyways?"

"Yours, 'course. I was just sayin' what they do in the movies or those detective books I got."

"This ain't no movie or story book." Hutch looked up at the sheriff again. "Wadn't a lot of fun...Some redneck old farmer seen me near where old lady Riggs was kilt."

"Is he still a suspect, Sheriff?"

He frowned. "Well, sort of. We call it person of interest."

I glanced at Hutch. "Huh, I can tell you there's not a lot interestin' 'bout him."

He thumped me again. "That's not what he means, dummy."

§§§

CHAPTER TWO

WARE ROAD

"Eder? Eder? Are you here?"

The plump, somewhat dowdy, middle-aged woman pushed the front door open and stepped inside the musty, overheated frame house. She carried a metal tray covered with a patterned dish towel made from a feed sack.

"Eder, you're not takin' a nap are you?...I brought you some dinner."

She glanced around the living room lit only by a single bulb fixture in the center of the ceiling. Books were scattered about the floor in a haphazard manner and a glass dust catcher lay in pieces on the floor in front of the bookcase.

The woman frowned and headed into the kitchen. She screamed and dropped the tray, shattering the bowl containing hot Irish stew.

The mixture of meat and vegetables spread across a wide area of the linoleum with some splattering on the bodies of a small black dog and an elderly man—both were lying side by side, dead on the floor, in large puddles of blood.

The woman held her hand over her mouth, trying not to vomit, as she backed out of the kitchen to the living room.

A younger woman, her daughter, came rushing in the front door after hearing the scream as she sat in the car in front of the porch.

UNION COUNTY

"What is it, Mama?"

Her mother, Idabell Warren, pointed toward the kitchen as she continued to back away from the door.

"He's...he's dead, Lulu. Eder's dead...his poor little dog too...Oh, my God in Heaven, who would do such a thing?"

"We've got to go call the sheriff, Mama, don't touch nothin', we'll drive over to Aunt Myrtle's, she's the closest, an' use her phone."

"But the mess?"

"Leave it...Come on."

Idabell looked back over her shoulder to the kitchen as her daughter opened the front door. "Such a shame. Eder was so nice to talk with."

SHERIFF'S OFFICE - UNION COUNTY

"Now, Idabell, settle down and tell me what happened...slowly, please."

Sheriff Wilson leaned forward and grabbed a yellow pad on his desk and pulled it in front of him along with a pencil.

"Uh-huh...Eder Ross you say? On Ware Road?...Dog, too?...Uh-huh. I understand. You didn't touch anything, did you?...All right, I'm on the way. Ya'll stay put, hear?...Oh, and thanks for lettin' me know...Right. I know you are....Yes, Ma'am...Goodbye."

He disconnected by placing the black receiver in the cradle of the Bell rotary phone on his desk. "Mason, get in here."

Deputy Mason Brooks opened the door and came in. "Yessir?"

"Call Doctor Duckworth and tell him to meet me outside the front of the hospital...bring his bag and have Pete and Charlie bring the meat wagon...Got another dead one out on Ware Road other side of Three Creeks."

"Yessir, who is it?"

"Eder Ross."

"Golly. He's that Spanish American War veteran, ain't he?"

UNION COUNTY

Sheriff Wilson nodded as he slipped his jacket on and donned his Stetson. "Yeah...Rode with Teddy up the hill."

"Good gosh."

"Now, Mason, do it now!"

"Oh, yessir." He spun on his heel and headed back to his desk in the front office as the sheriff stomped out the door.

HAYNESVILLE ROAD

Sheriff Wilson's black county vehicle, with the gold sheriff's badge on the door with Union County Sheriff's Department under it, roared out the Haynesville Road. The single red light on top of the roof was flashing and the siren wailing.

JAMISON HOME

Most of us were in the parlor, warmin' at the fire. Me an' Hutch had just brought in some more firewood for the box when we heard the siren outside.

We ran to the front door with grandpa an' daddy right behind us as the sheriff pulled up at the front of the home and stopped. The World War II surplus ambulance the county bought stopped right behind him.

The sheriff opened his door, leaving one foot inside on the floorboard and turned toward grandpa standin' on the porch.

"Come go with us, John. Looks like we got another robbery an' killin'...Eder Ross over on Ware Road."

"Let me get my coat, Myron." He turned toward daddy. "Grab yours, Joe, go with us."

"You say so." He turned to follow John inside.

"Can we go, Daddy?"

"Expect, not, Foot, ya'll better stay here. Doubt the sheriff wants a crowd at a murder scene."

Me an' Hutch looked at each other. We both said, "Dang." As daddy disappeared back inside.

UNION COUNTY

We went inside, too, an' got in front of the fire. Bobby was in our bedroom, takin' a nap. Mama said that teenage boys took a lot of naps. I didn't understand it, but guess I would one day when I became a teenager.

I had got in the habit of carryin' a small spiral ring notepad in my pocket—pulled it out 'long with a stubby #2 yella pencil.

"What's that for?"

I looked at Hutch an' realized I was goin' to have to explain some things to him. "I been readin' these books, Hutch…"

"Well, heck, Foot, good for you."

"Not what I mean, dipstick."

He wrinkled his forehead. "Then what?"

"Been readin' these books 'bout these brothers…Frank an' Joe Hardy. Their daddy's a detective an' they're learnin' how to be sleuths, too. Got a different crime in each book."

"What's a sleuth?"

I raised one eyebrow at him. "It's a person that investigates a crime."

"Oh, like a cop or detective?"

"Yeah, but private-like." I grinned. "That's what we're gonna do. Can't have folks just goin' 'round blamin' coloreds just because."

"Just because what?"

"Just because they're coloreds or Indians, or even Japs...Ain't right."

"Oh...yeah."

"Only have one of the books with me. I'll let you read it."

"Jammin'! What's it called?"

"The title is, *Footprints Under the Window* by a Franklin Dixon, in 1933."

"Wow, that was a long time ago."

"You think?"

Hutch cocked his head at me. "Just said so, didn't I?"

I rolled my eyes. "It's just an expression."

"Of what?"

I shook my head. "Never mind."

"What say we ride our bikes over to that Miz Riggs house an' see if there might be some signs outside the house the killer might have left that the sheriff missed?"

I shook my head. "Think we oughta wait a day or two till it warms up. It's too dang cold with that north wind a blowin' to ride bicycles...specially with no gloves."

"Is bein' back in a big town makin' you a titty baby?"

"Naw, but I been there, done that. Tried to ride my bike at home up in Colorado one Saturday mornin' to football practice, it wadn't cold as it is here...Didn't make it. Had to turn around an' go back home. Hands got so cold I couldn't feel the grips on my handlebars."

"No lie?"

"No lie...Had icicles hangin' off my chin from my nose runnin' time I got back to the house."

"Uh-uh."

"Uh-huh...did so."

"Dang!...Guess we'll wait."

"We'll see what we can get out of daddy an' grandpa on what happened at that Mister Ross' place when they get back...Betcha it's the same person that's doin' the crimes."

"No bet."

CRIME SCENE

Sheriff Wilson pulled up in front of the Ross modest shiplap sided residence. Pete and Charlie pulled in beside him. They got out as the sheriff, Doctor Duckworth, John, and Joe did.

"Ya'll wait out here till the doc is through doing his thing, Pete...You know how the old quack is."

"Yessir."

"I'll old quack you...dang tin horn imitation lawman."

"Imitation, my foot."

The sheriff opened the front door. The inside was still hot because the propane gas space heater hadn't been shut off.

"Just as well turn that thing off, John. No need for it now."

"Yeah, got it."

He turned the handle on the side of the heater sideways and in less than ten seconds, the smokeless blue flame burning inside against the asbestos back went out.

The sheriff and Doctor Duckworth entered the kitchen where the bodies of Eder and his little dog were. John and Joe took the opportunity to inspect the front room.

The doctor squatted down, checked Eder's nonexistent pulse as a matter of course, then slipped on a pair of surgical gloves and palpated the blood matted hair on the back of the man's head—he nodded.

"What I figured...blunt force trauma. Caved the skull in...Death was pretty much instant." He glanced at the small dog. "Same for the pup."

"Anyway to tell what the murder weapon was?"

The doctor shook his head. "Something hard and round, Myron...Same as Miz Riggs." He spread his fingers across the indentation. "About the size of a baseball bat...Wouldn't be surprised but that's what it was."

Sheriff Wilson puffed his cheeks and blew his breath out. "Poor devil. The killer must have gotten inside and slipped up behind him. Eder was dang near deaf...Don't think he'd heard it thunder for ten or fifteen years. Think he was probably too close to the cannons or mortars in the war. Ruined his hearing."

"War?"

"Yeah, he fought in the Spanish American War."

"Ah, with Teddy...Would make sense."

Back in the living room, Joe bent over looking at the books pulled out of the bookcase.

"Huh, that's interestin'."

"What's that?" John leaned over to see what Joe was pointing at.

These books weren't just pulled off the shelves."

"What do you mean?"

"They were taken out one at a time, opened, then thrown to the floor...They're all open, see?" He looked up at John. "They were lookin' for something stuck inside one of these books."

"Wonder what?"

Joe pursed his lips. "That's the sixty-four dollar question, John."

§§§

CHAPTER THREE

JAMISON HOME

"Wow, Foot, this is nifty fat city." Hutch looked up from the Hardy Boys book I lent him. "We can do this."

Think he'd heard those words from some older boys at his school—didn't use 'em last summer.

UNION COUNTY

We were layin' on a big rag rug grandma had made in front of a roarin' fire in the fireplace.

Tiny was curled up between us, soakin' up the heat, too—way too dang cold to sit out on the front porch.

"Yeah, but you gotta bear in mind, knucklehead, that you're readin' a book an' we're dealin' with real life...but maybe we can learn some good stuff from Frank an' Joe."

"I'm not a knucklehead."

"Are too."

"Am not."

"Are too."

"Am not."

"How come?"

"How come what?"

"How come you think you're not a knucklehead?"

"How come you think I am?"

"Well, you're a knucklehead if you think Frank an' Joe are real."

He frowned. "They could be."

"Huh...may have a point. Okay, you're not a knucklehead."

"See."

"Today."

He thumped me. Tiny looked up for a second, then laid her head back down an' promptly closed her eyes again. I thumped him back.

We both looked up as car doors slammed outside.

"Must be the sheriff, daddy, grandpa, an' the doc back from that robbery an' killin'."

Hutch glanced over at me. "Got your note pad ready?"

"Yeah, but need to remember what they say, don't want to be too obvious 'bout takin' notes...might get all bent outta shape."

"Why?"

"On account daddy's gonna think we're stickin' our nose in murders an' stuff."

"Well?"

"Hush."

UNION COUNTY

We heard the front door close an' everbody came in the parlor an' headed to the fireplace.

Grandma came in the other door from the dinin' room. Figured she was gonna see if they wanted coffee—probably no need in askin'.

She looked at grandpa an' he nodded—yep, no need at all.

In a minute, her an' mama came in with four cups of coffee in thick white mugs. Grandpa an' Doctor Duckworth had already sat down in rockers after warmin' their backsides for a minute. The sheriff an' daddy weren't too far behind.

I glanced at Hutch an' kinda nodded.

He rolled up on one elbow an' turned to the sheriff. "Does this mean I ain't on the list no more, Sheriff Wilson?"

"Well, kinda looks that way, Hutch. Kinda looks that way."

He grinned big an' looked back at me.

"Was this one the same as the others, Sheriff?"

"I'd say pretty much, Foot." He glanced at grandpa.

"What about Mister Ross' little dog? What's gonna come of her?"

The sheriff looked back at Hutch. "She was killed too, Hutch."

"Awe...She was real sweet...Did, uh...ya'll bury her?"

Daddy nodded. "I did...Buried her out under that apple tree that was out front."

Hutch shook his head. "Don't understand it...just don't."

"What's that, son?"

"She wouldn't hurt nobody...Would never even bark when some of us would go by there to see if we could have an apple when they were gettin' ripe."

Grandpa nodded. "Looked like they killed her out of pure meanness...she wasn't any bigger than Tiny."

Tiny raised up her head when grandpa mentioned her name, then laid back down when it didn't look like he wanted anything.

"She was probably in the way when they were goin' through Mister Ross' books."

I looked at Hutch, then back to daddy. "Goin' through his books? What kind?"

He looked at me. "Don't think they were interested in the kinds of books, Hoss Fly, they were mostly what are called the classics, like *The Iliad* and *The Odyssey* by Homer...real heavy stuff, but there were a few mysteries. Think they were looking for something inside one of them."

"You mean like a treasure map or somethin'?"

"Got no idea, Slicknickle. No idea at all."

I looked at Hutch. "Sure would like to see some of those books."

"Yeah, me too."

Daddy looked at the sheriff. "Know how you like books, all right."

The sheriff raised his eyebrows. "Well, old Eder Ross didn't have any next of kin I know about...Maybe we can work something out."

"Wow! Reckon how many of 'em there are?"

The sheriff looked at daddy an' grandpa.

They glanced at each other.

"Going to just make a swag, Hoss Fly, an' say forty or fifty, wouldn't you, John?"

"Fair close, Joe."

"Gol-uh-olee!"

Doctor Duckworth leaned over to the sheriff. "What's a swag?"

"Scientific wild-ass guess."

"Oh, right. Knew that...Just forgot."

"Uh-huh...You wouldn't have remembered that if it bit you on the butt, you old quack." The sheriff looked at the doc over the tops of his wire-rimmed glasses.

"I'll quack you, dang tin horn excuse for a lawman."

"You'll think tin horn you..."

Nobody paid them any attention on account they'd been best friends since grade school.

We could all hear the sound of a car door closin', then in a minute, there was a knock at the front door. Tiny jumped up with that rapid fox terrier bark of hers...rar...rar...rar...rar, an' ran to the dog run. She stopped in front of the door barkin' at some guy on the porch.

Grandpa got up an' got there 'bout the same time as grandma comin' from the kitchen, but she opened the door which was a kinda frosted patterned glass halfway down. "Yes?"

Me an' Hutch had run up behind grandpa. The man on the porch was in some type of brown uniform with one of those flat-topped military style hats. He took it off when grandma opened the door.

"How do you do, madam. I'm Fabien Fontenot with LeRoux Brothers Coffee. We're settin' up routes in Arkansas an' Louisiana for our new coffee blends an' other sundries folks might need...Just droppin' by our catalogue with our list of products an' prices."

He held out the flyer type thing. Grandma opened the screen door an' took it. "Thank you, Mister Fontenot, we trade pretty regular with Stanley Coffee people."

"Yes, Ma'am. Good folks, too." He held out a sample bag of coffee. "Like I mentioned, we have some new coffee blends...Just wanted to drop off a sample for you to try."

She opened the door again, took the small bag an' looked at the front. "Dark roast with chicory." Grandma looked back up at him. "Louisiana style coffee?"

"Yes, Ma'am."

"Well, we do like our coffee strong. We'll give it a try."

"Appreciate it, Ma'am. I'll drop back by in a week or so an' see if ya'll like it."

She looked back at grandpa. He nodded.

"Thank you...Mister Fontenot."

"My customers just call me Fabien, Ma'am."

Grandma smiled an' nodded. "Fabien it is, then...We're the Jamisons. This is my husband John an' I'm Mame."

He put his hat back on an' touched the short plastic brim with his fingers. "Yes, Ma'am, nice to meet ya'll. Have a nice day, hear?"

He turned an' headed back out toward his light brown Ford van with LeRoux Brother's Coffee painted on the side in gold letterin'. There was another fella sittin' in the front waitin'. Guess they worked in pairs.

Grandma closed the front door. "Nice young man." She looked at the price sheet in the catalogue, then held up the bag. "We'll try this. They're a little cheaper than Stanley."

Grandpa nodded. "Uh-huh...Cheaper's not always better, Mame."

Grandma cocked her head a little to the right. "I know that John L. Franklin." She turned an' headed back toward the kitchen.

Grandpa glanced down at me an' Hutch. "I probably shouldn't have said that." He thought for a minute. "Give you boys a little advice on handling women, 'specially when you get married...There's two words you'll be well served to remember that will guarantee a good and happy relationship."

"What're those, Grandpa?"

He looked at grandma's back goin' through the door to the kitchen down the hall, then back down at us. "Yes, dear."

§§§

CHAPTER FOUR

JAMISON HOME

"Hey, hey, ya'll come look...it's snowin'!" Hutch stood at the window of the parlor that looked out on the front porch an' yard. "Gol-uh-olee! The flakes comin' down 're near big as a half-dollar."

I came over beside him to watch, too. Had been seein' a lots of snow up in Colorado—but this was different.

"Wow, don't see nothin' like those up at home. It usually snows sideways an' the flakes are a bunch smaller."

"How come?"

"Don't know. Way God wants it, I guess."

Wadn't takin' long for those big ol' flakes to cover the ground. Couldn't hardly see grandpa's barn out front cross the road down to Unka J.B.'s.

"Hey, Foot, let's go outside an' see as we can catch some on our tongues."

"You boys put your coats on first."

"Okay, Grandpa."

"Keeps snowin' like this an' we'll make some snow ice cream."

"Hot diggidydog." I nudged Hutch an' we both got big grins.

"While you're out there, go across the way there an' throw Sally and Ted an' extra flake of hay. They may need it this afternoon...an' check their water, make sure it's not froze over."

"Yesssir."

Sally an' Ted were grandpa's Guernsey milk cow an' his big ol' black-nosed Tennessee plowin' mule. Grandpa'd left 'em in their stalls in the barn on account he figured it was gonna snow—he was right. 'Course he usually is.

Me an' Hutch had our coats on an' I pulled my black wool watch cap down over my ears. "Ain't you got no cap?"

He shook his head.

"Just a minute." I ran into Bobby an' my bedroom an' came back out with another cap. "Here, this watch cap is yours...got two, can't wear but one at a time."

Hutch looked at the soft knitted wool, an' then pulled it over his short nappy hair an' his ears like I did. "Wow, this is nifty, Foot, thanks...How come they call 'em 'watch caps'?

"Guess 'cause the Navy guys wear 'em on ships when they're standin' watch at night...What Unka Dorris tol' me, an' he was in the Navy in the war."

"Were these in the war?"

I shrugged. "Don't know. Could have been...Got 'em at the Army Navy Surplus store at home. Everbody wears 'em back in Colorado in the winter...keeps your ears warm."

He put his hands over the cap on top of his ears. "I'll say...How much were they?"

"Just a dollar apiece."

"Got a dollar, let me pay you for it."

I whacked his shoulder. "Naw, goose...what are friends for?"

He grinned an' whacked me back, but not near as hard as I did him—thought he was gonna cry for a second. Guess he doesn't have any close friends like me in that colored school where he goes in Junction City.

We went to the front door, Tiny was followin', but she stopped after gettin' halfway out on the porch, stuck her nose in the air, turned around, an' went back inside—guess she wasn't havin' any part of it.

Me an' Hutch headed down the steps of the stoop to the yard. The big ol' flakes were almost makin' a splatin' sound when they hit our faces.

Hutch stuck his tongue out an' one the size of a quarter landed smack in the middle. He pulled it back in his mouth.

"Wow, that was neat." He stuck it out again.

I did the same an' got two, one right on top of the other. We both giggled.

"Bet it won't be ten minutes 'fore we can make snowballs. Let's go ahead an' feed Sally an Ted."

The barn was gettin' hard to see on 'count the flakes were hittin' us in the eyes—had to keep 'em kinda squinted an' hold our heads down as we made our way to the barn.

"Hope it don't get like up in Colorado."

"How's that?"

"It can snow so hard an' heavy some times that daddy has to string a rope 'tween the house an' the garage so we don't get lost."

"Really?"

"Uh-huh. Everthing just gets so that you can't see...the natives call it a 'white-out'. Like bein' inside a cotton ball."

"No kiddin'?"

"No kiddin'."

We got inside an' left the door open a tad so we could get a little light. I stepped over to the stack of bales, one was already busted, so I grabbed a good flake 'bout six inches thick an' handed it to Hutch.

"Give this one to Sally."

I got another just the same an' dropped it over in the stall into Ted's manger—think he was gettin' a mite hungry 'cause he dove right in. Checked his water an' there was only a thin film of ice on it. Broke it with my fist. Could hear Hutch doin' the same over at Sally's stall next to Ted's.

Hutch musta heard a noise over between the hay an' the wall of the barn 'cause he turned that way. "What's that?"

"What's what?"

We both listened at the repeated soft cry.

§

Joe looked out the window toward the barn. "Really gettin' heavy out there, but not like up in Colorado."

"What do you think we've gotten?"

"About two-three inches so far, I'd say, John, and still comin' hard."

He chuckled. "Watch 'em head straight to the fire when they come back in."

Joe laughed back. "I'm sure...Here they come, all hunched over against the wind."

§

Me an' Hutch hustled from the gate to the porch—was gettin' even harder to see. I opened the screen door, then the main one. He went through first while I closed it behind us.

We boogied straight to the fire. I started shuckin' my coat an' hat. Hutch just opened his an' stood close so the black an' white ball of fur under his coat could get warm.

Tiny was layin' in her spot in front of the fire. She looked, then got up an' put her front feet on Hutch's leg, tryin' to get a better view.

"Want me to hold him, Hutch, while you peel out of your coat an' hat?"

He looked at me, then down at the pup an' shook his head. "Uh-uh. Let me warm him up first...He's shakin' like a leaf."

Grandpa leaned forward in his rocker. "Whatcha got there, buttercup?"

"It's a puppy, Grandpa. It was tryin' to keep warm out in the barn. Somebody musta thrown him out over to the Haynesville Road...Just like they did Tiny up in Sulfur, Oklahoma, when she was a pup...He's scared an' cold."

"So I see." He looked at daddy. "Joe would you go see if Mame could warm up some milk for the little fella. That'll help him almost as much as the fireplace...and Hutch."

"Sure thing, John, could use some coffee myself...You?"

"Now that you mention it." He looked at me an' Hutch. "Maybe the boys would like some hot milk, or cocoa?"

"I'll take some hot milk, Daddy."

"Me too, Mister Joe...after he gets his."

Hutch glanced down at the puppy who looked like he was warmin' up some—wadn't shakin' quite as much.

"Unless I miss my guess, I'd say the little fella is mostly border collie."

Hutch looked over at grandpa. "Really?...Hear they're real smart dogs."

"Looks like you've a mind to keep him."

He smiled an' looked down again when the pup licked his hand. "Sure can't put him back outside...He's too little."

"No, I expect not...What are you going to call him?"

"You said you thought he was border collie...How 'bout Lassie, like the movie star dog?"

"Lassie is a girl, dufus."

He looked at me. "Oh, right...Well, how 'bout Laddie, then?"

I raised my eyebrows an' nodded. "Works for me."

Tiny gave a short bark at Hutch tellin' him she wanted to see. He bent over an' held Laddie out toward her.

She sniffed of his nose, then licked it.

I grinned. "Looks like he passes Tiny's smell test...bet they get along."

"I'll bet she tries to mother him...Watch an' see."

"Think so, Grandpa?"

"I do...Set him down in front of her, Hutch. He looks like he's warmed up enough."

Hutch set Laddie down. He wasn't quite as big as Tiny, but he'd be a lot bigger in a few months, I 'spect.

He sniffed of her an' Tiny did the full circuit of Laddie, 'cludin' the butt sniff, then they started lickin' each other's faces. Tiny danced around in front an' the side of him, wantin' to play. He flopped over on his back, wigglin', an' wavin' all four feet in the air. Yep, no question, they were gonna get along. Amazin' how quick dogs can figure out they're gonna like someone or someplace—even puppies.

Grandma an' mama came in with the hot milk for me, Hutch, an' Laddie, an' coffee for grandpa an' daddy.

She set a shallow pan down in front of the fireplace an' Laddie's nose. He stuck his head over inside, sniffed an' right away went to lappin' it up. Tiny waited a second, then joined in. There was enough for the both of 'em.

"That's the coffee that young man left. How do you like it?"

Grandpa took a sip, kinda raised one eyebrow an' wrinkled his face. "Oooo, taste's like seed ticks smell."

Now since I don't know what seed ticks smell like it didn't mean much—for some reason I don't get ticks or chiggers like Hutch does. But sounds like that coffee might be a tad bitter.

"It's the chicory, John. We had to drill some wells a few years ago down at Lake

Charles, Louisiana. This is the way the folks down there drink it...It's stout, all right."

Grandpa took another sip. "Could use it for paint remover, I guess."

§§§

CHAPTER FIVE

TUBAL ROAD

"Think we'd best stop the reconnoitrin' for the day. Leave too many tracks with this snow."

"Got a point...Let's head to the house, then. Don't know about you but I could use some coffee an' somethin' to eat."

The driver nodded. "Yeah, I'm for that...Atlanta Road is a little further this way, we can turn there."

"Somebody around here has got to have it."

"Agree...no other way they could have gone to get there."

JAMISON HOME

Tiny an' Laddie had fallen asleep, all twined up together, in front of the fire.

I looked over at Hutch. "Let's go get a pot an' a couple big spoons from grandma, go outside, an' fill it with some of that snow."

He was standin' lookin' out the front window. "Yeah, looks like 'bout seven or eight inches an' it's still fallin'."

"We can scoop it off the hood of daddy's Ford. Won't get no dirt that way."

"Good idea. Hate it when you get grit when you're eatin' it."

"Come on...One thing about it."

"What?"

"Snow's fresh enough won't be any yella stuff on it."

"Yella?...Oh, right." Hutch giggled.

"That's one of the first things they told us in school up in Colorado...Don't eat yella snow."

"Yuck."

We put on our coats again an' the caps an' headed down to the kitchen.

"Grandma, can we have a pot an' some spoons? Grandpa said we should make some snow ice cream when there was enough..."

"An' there's near seven inches now an' still fallin'."

She looked from me to Hutch, then nodded an' glanced at mama. "We'll beat up some eggs and mix in the sugar and vanilla flavoring while ya'll are filling the pot...get plenty."

"Yessum, we will."

Mama handed me a big ol' blue speckled graniteware pot an' gave Hutch a couple of mixin' spoons.

We turned, ran back down to the front door, an' out on the porch. The flakes weren't near as big as before. Guess it's like when it starts to rain, the first drops are humongous, then they back off an' get regular—but it was still comin' down heavy.

"Bet we get ten inches or better 'fore it's done."

I looked at Hutch. "You reckon?"

"Seen it do this a couple times last year."

"Maybe we can make a snowman tomorra...if it stops."

"Oh, it'll stop awright, never seen it snow more'n a day before."

"It can snow for two or three days up in Colorado...call it a blizzard. We can get a foot, or even two."

"Really?"

"Yep."

We went down the steps of the stoop an' trudged through the snow to the gate. Daddy's car was parked just outside near the sycamore trees—they were bare as old Mother Hubbard's cupboard.

Hutch handed me one of the big spoons an' we went to scrapin' the snow from the hood. It was a good eight inches now an' still comin' down pretty hard.

§

Didn't take no time an' we had that pot full an' piled up high like a snowcone. I handed Hutch my spoon so I could carry it by both handles. Surprisin' how much snow can weigh.

We got back inside an' headed down the wide hallway to the kitchen. It wadn't a whole lot warmer in it than it was outside but it would be when we got in the kitchen on account of grandma's big ol' wood burnin' cook stove. It was fired up 'cause she an' mama were cookin' up a ginormous pot of venison sausage Irish stew an' cornbread for supper.

Hutch opened the door to the kitchen for me since both my hands were occupied. We went in an' I set the pan of snow on the counter. Grandma had already put out a big ceramic bowl for the mixin' an' next to it was a small bowl of beat-up eggs, sugar, vanilla flavorin' an' a cup of pure cream. It was time.

Grandma grabbed her wooden mixin' spoon, poured some of the mix in the ceramic bowl an' turned to me. "Put three or four big spoons of snow on top, there, Foot."

"Yessum."

I dumped 'em in an' she started mixin'—foldin' the snow into the eggs, sugar an' stuff.

"More."

She added some more mix. "More snow."

I kept addin' snow an' she kept addin' the mix an' cream till it was all together. She stirred it around a bit an' it looked almost like that soft ice cream you can get at the Dairy Mart, just not quite as smooth—um-um, sure smelled good.

Mama had some small bowls an' spoons already on a wood tray an' she started fillin' 'em with snow ice cream—even one for Tiny an' Laddie.

Grandma set what was left in the ceramic bowl on a shelf outside next to the back door where it would stay froze.

Me an' Hutch carried our own while mama an' grandma came behind us with daddy's, grandpa's, Bobby's, an' the dogs as we went into the parlor.

Everbody got their bowls, Tiny an' Laddie really went to town on theirs. When we'd go to a Dairy Mart back home, always had to get Tiny her own nickel cone of ice cream. She'd pester you to death if you didn't.

Grandpa nodded as he took a bite. "Um, sure good. Thanks boys for goin' out and scoopin' the snow up." He looked at grandma an' mama. "An' ya'll done a bang-up job with the mixin's, too."

I had a grin that spread across my face. "Looks like Tiny an' Laddie kinda like it, too."

I turned to daddy 'cause a thought ran through my head like they seem to tend to do from time to time. "Daddy, did any of those books in the floor over at Mister Ross' house stand out or maybe you noticed more'n some of the others?" That was one of those questions Frank or Joe Hardy would ask.

He paused for a moment with a spoonful in the air, then went ahead an' stuck it in his mouth before he nodded. "Now that you mention it, Foot, there was one, why?"

"Oh, just curious, is all. Thought it was strange   that some ne'er-do-well would be lookin' through books."

Hutch looked up from his bowl. "What if it was more'n one?"

"Then it would be ne'er-do-wells, peckerwood, but still strange." I looked back at daddy. "What was it?"

"His family Bible was sorta on top of the other books, like it was the one looked at last...or the most."

I ate another bite an' then got the brain freeze, an' squenched up my face till it passed. "Mmm-mmm, that smarted, best slow down a little." I looked back at daddy. "What page was it opened to?"

"That's another interesting question, Hoss Fly...It was open to the family page, the one that lists the family tree...so to speak."

Grandpa looked up. "That would be pretty specific, Joe...A little beyond chance it would just fall open to that page...You think that whoever opened it wanted to see who the rest of Eder's family was?"

Daddy's eyebrows went up. "Makes sense to me, John."

"When we can get out, need to go back over there and check. Sheriff Wilson said Foot an' Hutch could have what they wanted of the books, anyway...We'll load 'em up and bring them over here, especially that Bible..."

"Think we need to see who all is on that family tree...If I don't know 'em..." He looked at grandma. "...Mame will."

She nodded. "Most likely. Both our families have been in this area for six generations or more."

"Got a hunch, John?"

"Maybe."

§§§

CHAPTER SIX

ATLANTA ROAD

"Hey, hold it." The passenger pointed at the house on the right side of the dirt road. "Don't look like anybody's home at the Worley place. The old lady that lives there is the right age, too...Just as well stop an' check it out while we're here.

We're only a couple hundred yards from the Haynesville Road."

"Ah, gotcha. There'll be more tracks in the snow on the main road...ours'll be lost in the shuffle."

"There you go."

The driver pulled into the front yard, stopped, and they got out.

"Get the bat, might be a dog in the house or somethin'."

"Right."

The other man reached back inside the vehicle, got the beat-up Louisville Slugger from behind the front seat, and the two stomped through the snow up to the porch.

The first man knocked on the door, just to make sure no one was home, while his friend held the bat alongside the back of his leg, out of sight.

He reached for the doorknob after a few short moments figuring the house was, in fact, empty, but the door opened before he could turn the knob.

"Yes?" An eighty year old woman in a worn, pale green chenille house coat stood inside the doorway.

The man in front of the door started, surprised. "Oh, wasn't sure anyone was home."

"What do you want?"

He looked at his friend who just shrugged, turned back and shoved the old woman back into the house. She fell backward to the floor with a groan.

The other man stepped inside, behind the first, swung the bat like a golf club, smacking her on the side of the head with a sickening crunch. She jerked several times and the heel her left house shoe clad foot drummed briefly on the worn carpet covering the hardwood floor—then was still. Blood slowly spread outward from her head, pooling and soaking into the old floor covering.

"Damn, didn't think anybody was home...Well, no never mind."

The first man pointed. "Looks like a bookcase over there."

He walked over, picked up the black, thick, well used, Bible where it laid on the top, and opened it to the family page in the front.

The other man looked over his shoulder and pointed. "There...Could be a possibility."

"Yeah." He ripped the two pages of the family tree from the Bible, stuffed them in his pocket, and threw the sacred book to the floor. "See anything else?"

"Wonder if there's anything in this jar?" He picked up the decorated ceramic vase, also on top of the book case, and lifted the lid. "Well, well."

"What?"

He held up a fistful of cash he'd pulled from inside as he pitched the jar to the floor where it shattered. "Supper money."

After wiping the bat on the old woman's house coat, he turned toward the door. "Let's go."

The two men went out the front door, closing it behind them, walked through the still falling snow, to their vehicle, and headed to the Haynesville Road. The wipers worked overtime sweeping the fresh snow away from the windshield.

JAMISON HOME

Grandma came in the parlor. "Dinner's ready, if ya'll want to eat...I can always throw it out."

We all jumped up play-like protestin' on account we knew she was kiddin' around. Grandmas are like that sometimes.

I elbowed Hutch. "Race you."

"Ah-ah-ah." Grandma wagged her finger at us. "I'll take a switch to the both of you."

We both grinned 'cause we were funnin' too. "Yessum."

Tiny was right on our heels an' Laddie was stickin' to her like glue as we walked to the dinin' room. Whatever she did, he was goin' to do.

The dinin' room was plenty warm. Long time ago, grandpa had put a vent behind grandma's cook stove that could be opened into the room—could be closed when it wadn't cold so it wouldn't get too hot in there.

Me, Hutch, an' Bobby took our places on the bench that ran 'long the dinin' table on the wall side—that's where the grand kids always sat. The grownups got chairs on the other with grandpa an' grandma at each end.

We waited till grandpa sat down first. Nobody told us to, just figured it was good manners. Tiny an' Laddie were under the table at me an' Hutch's feet.

Grandma brought out this big bowl of her special stew—she called it a tureen, don't know who named it that.

Mama carried out a big platter of cornbread an' a couple bowls of butter she had got from the icebox.

There were already bowls in front of each eatin' place an' we passed 'em one at the time down to grandma so she could fill 'em an' pass 'em back.

"Um-mm, sure smells good, Grandma."

"Thank you, Foot."

I looked at the thick stew an' could tell there was a whole bunch of pork an' venison sausage, 'long with taters, carrots, hominy, stewed tomatoes, cut okra, an' chopped onions in it. It was so thick you could stand your spoon up in the middle an' it wouldn't fall over.

Grandma called it real stick-to-the-ribs stew—not sure what that means. 'Course the cornbread was always good too, 'specially when you put a big slab of butter to melt in the middle, an' then dunk it in the stew.

Mama went back to the kitchen an' brought out a cloth covered basket of yeast rolls—like them too. Makes my mouth water just smellin' 'em cookin'.

But I been smellin' somethin' else. "Grandma, is that buttermilk pie I'm smellin' comin' from the kitchen?"

"You're getting good, Foot. Yes, it is."

Me an' Hutch looked at each other an' grinned.

"Oh, boy hidy."

She smiled back. "If ya'll eat all your supper."

Hutch nodded as he looked at his steamin' bowl. "Ain't no worries 'bout that Grandma Jamison...No worries atall."

I grinned big. "Uh-huh!" I took a big spoonful...

§

Me an' Hutch were both on our second slice of buttermilk pie. Tiny an' Laddie were lickin' our stew bowls down by our feet.

I ate the last bite an' wiped my mouth. "Grandma, we gonna have a Christmas tree?"

"Why of course, Foot. Figure ya'll can go cut one soon as the snow melts some."

"Got a nice grove of young white pine on the other side of the garden across the road...Some just the right size, too."

We glanced at grandpa, he always knew where the good trees were.

Grandma looked at Hutch. "Better take that pup out an' see if he'll do his business in the snow. Just as well start training him right."

"Like this, Hutch." I looked down at Tiny. "Wanna go outside, girl? Outside?"

She spun around twice an' woofed at me.

"See."

Hutch looked at Laddie. "Outside, Laddie?...Outside?"

He just looked at him an' cocked his head.

I swung my legs over the bench an' got up. "Come on, Tiny...outside." And headed for the hallway.

Hutch followed with Laddie prancin' along right on Tiny's heels. "Outside, Laddie."

We got out on the front porch. It had finally stopped snowin' an', sure enough, we got about ten inches. Really looked pretty—couldn't even see our tracks when we went out to get the snow for the ice cream earlier.

Didn't seem too cold on account there wasn't any wind, it was still an' quiet as a church mouse—nothin' was movin'.

We went down the steps to the yard an' buried up to past our ankles. Could tell Tiny was more used to bein' in snow 'cause of how much it snowed up at home, but Laddie was a different story. He sunk into the fluffy powder with just his head stickin' up—think he was confused.

Then he saw Tiny jumpin' up an' bouncin' through the snow, so he tried it. Couldn't jump very high but he could make a little headway.

Tiny squatted an' did her thing. Could tell 'cause of the steam risin' up from behind her rear.

I looked at Hutch. "There's your yella snow."

"Yuck."

Laddie jumped around a few more times, then a cloud of steam rose from his backside. He had squatted to pee, too, like all puppies do. When he gets grown, guess he'll learn to hike his leg to water a tree or somethin'.

"Awright, let's go back inside."

Even though the wind wadn't blowin' we were startin' to get cold 'cause we didn't take the time to put on our coats.

We tromped over to the steps an' climbed up to the porch. Tiny an' Laddie saw us an' bounced through the deep snow lookin' almost like some porpoises I had seen in one of those newsreels that has the big rooster at the beginnin' of 'em at the pitchur show—the rooster never made a lot of sense to me.

Laddie had to struggle some to get up the four steps but he got it done. He an' Tiny both shook the loose snow from their fur an' trotted over to the door as I opened it an' we went inside.

I nudged Hutch to congratulate Laddie.

"Oh, right. Good job, Laddie boy, good job."

He bent over an' ruffled the hair on his head. Laddie licked his hand an' flopped over on his back.

We went into the parlor an' laid down in front of the fire. Tiny an' Laddie got right between us as Hutch grabbed the Hardy Boys book an' opened it to the page he'd bookmarked.

He looked over at me. "Think there's somethin' in those folks Bibles the..." He looked down at the page in the book to get the word. "...perpetrators are lookin' for?"

"Think grandpa believes there is. But we need to take our own look-see when we can go over to Mister Ross' to pick us those books."

"Reckon we'll find anythin'?"

"Won't know till we look, Jaybird...Have learned one thing from all the crime an' detective books I've been readin'."

His forehead wrinkled. "Do I have to guess or are you gonna tell me?"

I grinned an' nodded. "A crime is usually committed on account of three reasons..."

"That would be?"

"Love...revenge..." I smiled again 'cause I had a hunch like grandpa. "...or money."

§§§

CHAPTER SEVEN

JAMISON HOME

I heard a car door close out front, jumped up an' ran to the front window in time to see Sheriff Wilson trudge through the snow to the front porch.

He rapped on the front door after stompin' the white stuff off his galoshes 'fore he reached down, unbuckled 'em an' pulled each off his shoes with the toe of the other foot.

Grandpa got to the door 'bout the same time. "Well, Myron, what brings you out in this mess...or do I have to ask?"

He nodded. "Yep, got a call from old Miz Worley's daughter-in-law. She went over to check on her when the snow stopped...found her inside the front door, head bashed in just like Eder Ross' an' Miz Riggs."

"Come on inside before you let what heat there is in this hall out...How did..."

Heard grandpa stop talkin' for a second, then he started back.

"Never mind...See the chains on your tires. Suspect you needed 'em."

"Did..."

"Have supper?"

"No, got the call just as I was settin' down to eat."

"Mame made a big pot of venison sausage stew and cornbread, plenty left...and maybe even a slice or two of buttermilk pie. Come on, we're havin' our after-dinner coffee."

"Oh, my. Sounds good. Got a bit of a chill goin' through the crime scene."

"Any tracks?"

"Just some dents left. Snow pretty well filled 'em up. Probably happened least a couple hours before it stopped.

Could hear 'em walk down the dog run to the dinin' room. I nudged Hutch.

"Let's go listen."

We got up and headed through the bedroom 'tween the parlor an' the dinin' room. Tiny an' Laddie were both fast asleep 'side each other in front of the fire.

Me an' Hutch sat down in the floor, Indian style, in the doorway to the dinin' room as grandpa an' the sheriff were sittin' down at the table.

"I'll get you a bowl of stew an' some cornbread, Myron. Want coffee?"

"Please an' thank you, Mame." He lifted up the cover over the basket in the middle of the table. "Oh, rolls."

UNION COUNTY

The sheriff grabbed one, slathered the top with butter an' took a big bite as grandma came back in from the kitchen with a hot bowl of stew. Mama brought out a small plate with a couple wedges of cornbread from the warmin' bin in the stove.

"Nobody makes yeast rolls like you do, Mame." He had another bite.

"Oh, pshaw, Myron Wilson."

"I mean it."

She looked over the tops of her wireless rimmed glasses at him, then smiled. "Well, thank you...Now enjoy your stew before you give us the bad news you came out to deliver."

"He's already told me the killer did the same to Miz Worley as he did to old Eder an' Miz Riggs."

"Oh, no, not another one."

The sheriff nodded as he ate a big spoonful of the stew. "'Fraid so...This time he tore the family pages out of her Bible an' took 'em...Umm, this is good, Mame."

Grandpa nodded. "Found some names on there that meant something, I'd say...Anything else?"

"Thank you, Myron...I think you were just hungry."

He shrugged, then swallowed. "A vase was shattered out a little away from her bookcase...Wasn't just knocked off to the floor, either. I'm surmising that's where she hid her ready cash."

Grandma cocked her head like she was thinkin'. "Have you noticed that all the folks that have been killed are within two or three years of being the same age?"

Grandpa looked over at her. "Huh...That's right, Mame, plus, they've all been within a half-mile of Haynesville Road."

The sheriff stopped with a slice of cornbread almost to his mouth an' looked at grandma, then at grandpa. "Son of a gun, that hadn't occurred to me. Too close to the forest to see the trees, reckon." He thought for another minute. "Just need to figure out what else has got them all connected."

"Something does, Myron...count on it." Grandpa took a sip of his coffee. "Got to be those names...Too bad we don't know what names were on those family pages."

The sheriff nodded. "Yeah." He went back to eating, then looked up. "Think we'll see if the daughter-in-law has any idea about the family tree that was on those pages."

I nudged Hutch. He nodded. We got up an' headed back to the parlor.

Tiny an' Laddie hadn't moved, but grandma told me dogs sleep a lot anyway. Guess that gives 'em more energy to play when they're awake.

We laid back down in front of the fire after I added a log to it—need to keep it goin'.

"Is this the only Hardy Boys book you brought?" He held up the copy of *Footprints Under the Window* I loaned him.

I nodded. "Yeah, didn't know we were gonna get involved in a bunch of murders an' stuff."

"How're we gonna solve it?"

"Beats me. The books always say that the criminals..."

"The perpetrators."

"Them too...leave somethin' behind or do somethin' dumb."

"What if they're geniuses or somethin' like that guy Sherlock Holmes is always after."

"You mean, Moriarty? How do you know 'bout Sherlock Holmes?"

"Had to read one of the books about him, *The Final Problem*, in English class this fall."

"Really?"

"Yeah, didn't understand all of it, but I remember the bad guy's name."

"Well, grandpa always says that people who break the law are usually not the brightest crayons in the box...will do somethin' stupid that gets 'em caught."

"Yeah, but how are we gonna know?"

I frowned at him. "If I knew that, then we would know 'head of time."

"Know what?"

I rolled my eyes at him. "That they did somethin' dumb...dipstick."

"Not bein' a dipstick, just pointin' out what you were sayin'."

"What?"

Hutch shook his head. "Never mind...You're givin' me a headache."

"Need an aspirin or a BC powder?"

"No...just change the subject."

"I did."

"Did what?"

"Changed the subject."

"Huh?"

"Asked if you wanted an aspirin or BC powder."

He thumped me an' I thumped him back.

Sheriff Wilson pushed back from the table. "Mame, gotta say don't know when I've had better stew...or buttermilk pie."

"Thank you, Myron, but you say that every time you eat here."

He winked at her. "Because it's true."

She grinned and shook her head as she picked up his dishes and carried them to the kitchen.

The sheriff turned his head. "John, why don't you and Joe come go with me."

"Uh-oh, what do you have in mind?"

"On the way out to Miz Worley's, I went by that juke joint on Haynesville Road...the Iddledo Club..."

"Uh-huh." John raised his eyebrow.

"Saw a couple of blue trucks parked in front."

"And?"

"Hutch said he saw two rednecks pass on the road in the direction of Miz Riggs house the day she was killed. They didn't see him 'cause he said he was down that branch a ways gathering paw-paw leaves for his grand mother, Mamie...Said couldn't tell much about them as their truck was stirring up dust, except it was a blue truck that was newer than old man

Green's Plymouth an' there was two of 'em...Might be a good time to check an' see if any of those blue trucks at the club have two guys ridin' around in it."

John nodded. "They're downing a few brews during the storm."

"Exactly."

John glanced at Joe. "You up for it?"

"I don't want to smell anything on ya'll's breath when you come back...I'll make you stay outside."

"Now, Mame, hon, when have you ever known me to go to a juke joint?"

"Just saying, is all."

Vertis turned to Joe. "Goes for you too, mister."

He grinned and winked at her. "Yes, dear."

"See you learned well, Joe."

"Figured that one out right at the get go, John."

The sheriff frowned. "What are ya'll talkin' about?"

John turned back to him. "The two words that almost guarantee a happy marriage..."

"Ah...'Yes, dear'."

"And don't ya'll forget it."

John looked back at Mame with a big grin. "Yes, dear."

§

Me an' Hutch walked back in the dinin' room as the sheriff's car drove off in the thick snow.

"Where was the sheriff, grandpa an' daddy goin', Mama?"

"Sheriff Wilson said he saw a truck like Hutch described at a club on the Haynesville Road when he was on the road where the lady that got killed lived. Went to check it out. Asked your daddy and mine to go along."

"Wow, wish we coulda gone."

Mama kinda squinted her eyes at me. Best not say no more.

UNION COUNTY

IDDLEDO CLUB

The sheriff pulled in to the side of the parking lot in front of the club. There were eight pickups and three cars out front. Only two of the trucks had chains—one was blue.

"Other blue truck must have left...Tire chains get the job done in this kind of snow...or even ice."

"Have to carry a set in my trunk all the time for up in Colorado. Get a lot worse snow up there than this, John."

"Can believe it."

Wilson turned in his seat to look at John, and then Joe in the back seat. "Tell ya'll what do. Don't need to go in there in a bunch. Some of them good ol' boys will bow up, think somethin's goin' on, an' we won't learn a thing."

"How do you want to do it, then, Myron."

"Think it would be all right if you an' Joe go in together. I'll follow in about five minutes."

"Ought to work...What do you think, Joe?"

"Juke joints are the same all over. 'Bout half of those boys will already be on the prod...especially if they've been in there most of the afternoon, soakin' up the suds durin' the storm."

John nodded. "Yup."

They got out, flipped up their collars, trudged to the front door, stomped the snow off, and opened it.

Every eye in the semi-dark club turned toward the door as it opened.

Joe glanced at John. "Uh-oh, don't see a friendly eye in the place."

"Now I know how a whore walkin' into a church feels."

§§§

CHAPTER EIGHT

JAMISON HOME

Hutch ran one finger down the center of the page he had opened in the Hardy Boy's book.

"Why do you do that?"

He looked up at me. "What?"

"Run your finger down middle of the page."

"Helps me to read the line."

"Reckon you need glasses?"

"Uh-uh...Don't think so. See the words okay. It just helps me keep my place."

"You sure?"

"Yeah. Just hadn't had as much practice as you. Readin' books is not somethin' they make a big to do 'bout in school."

"I probably read three times what they say to do in our school on my own."

"But you have more access to a library than me. They don't let coloreds in the one in Junction City."

"Well, that ain't right...Tell you what."

"What?"

"Whenever I get a book, I'll send it to you here at grandma an' grandpa's when I finish, you just have to promise you'll take care of 'em...Deal?"

Hutch got a grin that spread clean across his face as he nodded. "Deal."

"What chapter you on now?"

He glanced down. "Uh...twenty-two."

"Ah, gettin' to the good stuff."

"I know." He put his finger back in the middle an' started readin' again. "Says here they make a list of folks what could be the perpetrators."

"Suspect we need to do that."

IDDLEDO CLUB

Joe leaned over to John. "Ignore 'em."

"Yep."

"What're you gonna order?"

He grinned. "Well, you heard what our sweet wives said...You know, I'm not afraid of any man walking, but that little woman just scares me plumb to death."

Joe chuckled. "Yeah, I know exactly what you mean...But if we don't order a beer, the rowdies will dang sure take notice."

"Fact."

"Don't have to actually drink it...Came in to get out of the cold and talk, didn't we?"

"I'd say we did...or something like it."

They took seats at an empty table about halfway into the thirty by fifty cinderblock building. There was a potbellied stove a few feet further in—almost glowing. It was doing a good job of heating the room.

A rotund balding bartender approached their table. He had a dingy white apron tied around his waist and an equally dingy once white bar towel over his shoulder.

"What'll it be, gents?"

Joe looked up at him. "Got Lone Star?"

"Uh-huh...You from Texas?"

"On occasion."

"Have the same."

The bartender looked down. "Seen you a time or two over at Wortham's Feed Store...You're Big John Jamison, ain'tcha?...You're not from Texas."

"Been called that...And nope, just happen to like Lone Star."

He nodded. "Whatever suits you." The bartender strode back over to the bar and went behind it.

UNION COUNTY

One of the patrons got to his feet, strolled over to the big Wurlitzer juke box, put in some quarters, and started punching numbers on the front.

The strains of Hank Snow's, *I'm Moving On,* started blasting out of the speakers.

Joe looked at John. "Think that's a subtle hint?"

"Wouldn't be surprised."

"Back in Texas we call these kind of joints, gun an' knife clubs...If you don't have one when you come in...they'll rent you one." Joe sniffed the warm air. "Ever notice how every juke joint smells the same?"

"Well, haven't been to too many lately, but I'd say you're pretty close."

"Wonder if they buy the odor of stale cigarette smoke, piss, body odor, and vomit from a dealer or something?" Joe surreptitiously glanced around again. "Still gettin' the snake eye."

John nodded. "Even more so when they heard you say you were from Texas."

"Only said, 'on occasion'."

"Close enough."

The bartender brought two bottles of Lone Star over and set them on the table. "Be a dollar."

Joe pulled a dollar bill from his wallet and pushed it toward the barkeep. The man took it and headed back to the bar.

A rowdy at a nearby table glanced over at the bottles and turned to his friend sitting across from him. "Hear drinkin' Lone Star is 'bout the same as drinkin' stud horse piss."

Joe looked at John. "Here we go." He looked at the men at the other table. "Wouldn't know friend...never drank stud horse piss."

The man's head jerked up. "You sayin' I do?"

"Didn't say anything of the sort. Just said I wouldn't know...never tried it myself."

He turned to his friend. "He smart-mouthin' me, Billy?"

"Sounds kinda like it to me, Jimmy Jack."

"Think you smart-mouthed me, boy."

"One, I'm not your boy, an' two, I'm not sure you'd know the difference between smart-mouth and a statement of fact."

"Huh?"

Joe turned to John. "See?"

John shook his head. "Takes all kinds."

Jimmy Jack pushed his chair back and got to his feet. "You tryin' to test me, Texas mouth?"

Joe grinned. "Don't really think you'd pass any kind of test except maybe finger painting...Jimmy Jack."

He looked at Billy. "What'n hell's finger paintin'?"

Billy shrugged his shoulders. "Don't know. Why would anybody want to paint their fingers?"

Joe looked at John again. "See? That's two."

Jimmy Jack bowed up and stuck his chin out in Joe's direction. "Two what?...I'm fixin' to clean your plow, Texas mouth."

"Why don't you sit back down and drink your beer before you let your alligator mouth overload your jaybird ass."

Jimmy Jack turned to his friend. "He's pushin' me, ain't he, Billy?...Big tough Texan."

"If he ain't he's gettin' damn close to it, pard."

Jimmy Jack stepped over, cocked his fist, and swung at Joe's head all in one continuous motion. Joe leaned back without getting up, causing the redneck to miss.

He grabbed the front of the off balance man's shirt, and using his momentum at the end of his swing, propelled him completely over the table to somersault the floor on the other side. He landed flat on his back with a loud *thud* and a *whoosh* as all his air was forced from his lungs.

Billy grabbed his beer bottle by the neck, charged the table with it raised over his head only to meet John's ham-like fist as it buried up to the wrist in his pudgy stomach.

Billy's eyes bugged out as he dropped the bottle, fell to his knees, and folded over with his hands grabbing his middle. He toppled to the side in a fetal position.

Ten of the other eighteen drinkers in the club got up from their tables and headed toward the confrontation.

"Back up against the bar, John, so nobody can get behind us."

"Good idea."

They moved quickly to the bar, turned and backed up against it, an arm's length apart, as the ten belligerent local patrons charged forward to join in the fray.

A chair sailed in the air toward the pair. John easily knocked it aside with his thick arm.

The first man in the front swung a roundhouse at Joe. He blocked it with his left and countered to the center of the man's face with a vicious right jab—blood squirted from his smashed nose. The blow staggered him back where he fell into the two men behind him, taking all three to the floor.

The remaining seven crowded in a semicircle around Joe and John, too close to allow swings or open punches, and mostly getting in each other's way.

John grabbed one man directly in front of him and slung him toward Joe. "Here's one, take care of him, and I'll send another."

Joe snapped a left hook to the side of the man's head, dropping him to the floor, as John followed with another as promised.

Joe drove a pile driving jab to that one's stomach with a short counter uppercut to his chin—the man's eyes clicked back in his head, his knees buckled and he toppled backward. The juke box started playing Earnest Tubb's, *Goodnight Irene,* as he collapsed to the floor—but he didn't hear it.

Joe got a glancing blow to his left side before he head butted a big man in front of him, then kneed him in the crotch. The man squealed like a pig under a gate and dropped to his knees.

A little man, no more than 5'3", drove at John with his head down, pummeling his large stomach with both fists. John picked him completely off the floor and threw him over the heads of two other men in front of him to land on a table eight feet away, collapsing it to the floor.

Jimmy Jack finally got his wind back, picked up a broken table leg from the wreckage, and charged at Joe.

The three men who had fallen to the floor in a tangle with the first man Joe hit had gotten to their feet. They were all covered with the blood from the first man's busted nose. They moved cautiously back toward the still unscathed Joe and John.

Billy raised the table leg over his head, like a baseball bat, to swing at Joe.

The sheriff looked at the glowing numbers on his wrist watch. *Well, they should have had enough time to get a table and mingle a little with the other customers.* He exited his car and made his way through the ten inch deep snow to the door.

Sheriff Wilson opened it just in time to see the melee. Five men were already out on the floor in front of John and Joe backed up against the bar with another five trying to get to the pair. Some had bottles in their hands with one brandishing a knife.

The sheriff took notice of the man moving toward Joe with the broken table leg over his head. He drew his .38 Police Special, fired one round, striking the wooden leg just above the man's grip, shattering the wood, tearing it out of Jimmy Jack's hand, and sending pieces spinning across the room.

Instantly, everybody in the club froze in place at the boom of the sheriff's handgun in the confined space. Silence prevailed except for the last phrase of *Goodnight Irene—'I'll see you in my dreams'*, from the juke box.

UNION COUNTY

Sheriff Wilson's voice thundered out as he held his pistol pointed in the direction of the combatants. "What's the hell's all this then?" He looked at the bartender. "Bertrand...Speak up. Who started this?"

He pointed at Jimmy Jack, standing in the middle of the room, holding his hand. It wasn't bleeding, but it was numb from the impact of the bullet to the table leg.

"Jimmy Jack and Billy."

"Who's Billy?"

A redneck getting to his feet, bent over, still holding his stomach, meekly held up one hand.

The sheriff pointed. "You two, that table, sit down...Now." He looked at the five that were trying to surround Joe and John. "Ya'll drop them bottles and you, dumb shit, best get shed of that knife." He aimed his pistol at the man's head as he dropped it to the floor.

The two made their way to a table, pulled out chairs, and sat down while the others also did what they were told.

Sheriff Wilson walked over to John and Joe. "Ya'll all right?"

They both nodded. John grinned. "Nice shot, Myron."

He shrugged. "Actually I was aimin' for his arm."

§§§

CHAPTER NINE

JAMISON HOME

I had my yellow Big Chief tablet in front of me as we laid in front of the fire. Tiny and Laddie were still snugglin' together between us—snoozin' away.

"So who can we start with?" I licked the tip of a stubby #2 yellow pencil I had sharpened with my jack knife an' looked at Hutch waitin' for an answer. "You're the only one to have seen anything."

He had his elbows on the rug with his chin propped in his cupped hands. "Well, gotta go with them two rednecks I saw over near Miz Rigg's house to begin with."

I looked up at him. "Blue truck, right?"

"Uh-huh."

"Couldn't tell what kind, though?"

He shook his head. "Too much dust...but thinkin' back on it, believe it was shaped more like a Chevy than a Ford."

"That helps." I wrote that down, too. "Think of 'nbody else?"

"Only other person I seen was old man Green."

"Think he coulda done it?"

"Don't know...Looks mean enough to. 'Course that's when he's lookin' at me or another colored."

I licked my pencil again. "I'll write him down since he was close by, anyway...Nobody else you can think of?"

He shook his head. "Nope...Need to go see some of those other crime scenes when the snow melts."

IDDLEDO CLUB

The sheriff leaned back in his chair at the table. "All right, boys, why the ruckus?"

Jimmy Jack glanced at Billy, then back at Sheriff Wilson. "Aw, Sheriff, we wuz just funnin'."

"Wasn't very bright. A word to the wise...funning those two can get you hurt."

Both of them looked over at John and Joe at the next table, having cups of coffee, then looked down at the table top in front of them.

"Yessir, found that out," replied Jimmy Jack.

"Since you apparently don't know, John Jamison there is one of my deputies and Joe is his son-in-law visitin' from

Colorado. He's a driller for Shell Oil...on vacation."

Billy's eyes got big. "A driller...Good gosh amighty."

Jimmy Jack nodded. "Ain't nobody tougher in the oil patch than the driller."

Sheriff Wilson grinned. "That's putting it mildly...I'd say ya'll were dang lucky I got here when I did before they started mopping up the floor with you."

Both of them nodded.

"Ya'll wouldn't happen to be driving that blue Chevy out front...with the chains on the back tires, would you?"

They looked at each other.

Billy nodded. "Uh-huh...Why, did we do somethin'?"

"You tell me."

Once more they exchanged glances.

Jimmy Jack wiped his nose with the sleeve of his shirt. "Uh..."

"Where were you boys yesterday?"

"Oh, uh...we were just drivin' 'round...right, Billy?"

"Yeah, that's it...just drivin' 'round."

"You over on Sweet Road?"

Billy shot a quick glance at Jimmy Jack. "Uh...well, guess we coulda been."

"Whose truck is it?"

Jimmy Jack kind of raised his hand a little from the table top. "Uh...It's mine, Sheriff."

"Carry a rifle in your truck?"

"Well, uh...yeah. Don't everbody? Got a rifle an' a shotgun in my window rack."

"Maybe doing a little road huntin'?"

Billy and Jimmy Jack both looked at the table top again.

Billy raised his head. "Well, maybe. You know, case we see a wild hog or somethin'."

"Or something like a deer?"

Once more they exchanged glances.

"Stop by Miz Riggs' place?"

The color drained from both their faces.

"Uh...who?"

The sheriff squinted a little at Billy. "Riggs. Elderly widow woman...on Sweet Road."

"Uh...Naw, naw. Why would we want to stop there?"

The sheriff waited a couple of beats. "You tell me."

There was almost a full minute of silence as Sheriff Wilson looked first at Billy, then at Jimmy Jack.

Jimmy Jack's eyes cut to his left then back to the sheriff. "Uh...We don't even know the woman."

"Didn't ask if you knew her. Asked if you stopped by there."

Jimmy Jack's jaw muscles rippled. "Well, we didn't, okay?...Why you askin'?"

There was another almost minute of silence. "Because she's dead."

Jimmy Jack jumped to his feet. "You sayin' we killed her?"

"Didn't say anything of the sort...Now, sit down...What about Ware Road? What time did you drive down it?"

He twitched as he lowered himself back to his seat. "Uh...well it's hard to remember."

"Try."

He looked at his pal. "Well, guess we could have in the afternoon."

"Guess? Uh-huh."

The sheriff reached into his shirt pocket inside his coat and pulled out a small coil wire note pad. He opened it, laid a short pencil beside it, and pushed it toward Jimmy Jack.

"Write your addresses down. Don't leave the area in case I need to talk to you again...Wouldn't be real smart if I have to come lookin' for you...Understand?"

One more time they exchanged quick glances.

Jimmy Jack wrote down his address and shoved the pad and pencil in front of Billy. "Yessir."

Billy jotted down his information and looked up at his friend. "We just as well be goin', Jimmy Jack...Oughta be gettin' home."

"Yeah."

They got to their feet.

"Probably be a good thing, boys...Take care on the way. Still nasty out."

They both glanced over their shoulders at the sheriff, then at John and Joe, before they headed to the door.

Sheriff Wilson raised his hand at the bartender. "Cup of coffee, Bertrand...you don't mind."

"Comin' right up, Sheriff."

A patron punched a couple of buttons on the Wurlitzer—Lefty Frizzell's, *If You Got the Money I've Got the Time*, started playing.

Bertrand set a steaming white mug of black coffee in front of the sheriff, warmed up John and Joe's from the pot in his other hand, and walked back to the bar.

John looked at the sheriff and grinned. "That was masterful, Myron."

"What?"

"The way you handled those ne'er-do-wells."

Joe took a sip of his coffee and nodded. "Keeping 'em off balance by changing your line of questioning...makes me think you've done this before."

He returned the grin. "Once or twice...Think they were lyin' through their teeth."

John nodded. "Agreed."

The sheriff sipped at his own cup and set it back on the table and shook his head. "Got an' itch down the middle of my back...Somethin's just not right. I feel it."

John glanced at Joe. "You may have something there Myron. I'm not sure either one of those boys have enough sense to spit downwind."

Sheriff Wilson smirked. "You think?"

Bob Wills' *Faded Love*, picked up when the Lefty Frizzell song finished.

The sheriff noticed the song. "Odd how quick things can get back to normal in these places."

A couple of bundled up ladies came in the front door as if to typify his statement.

John turned to the sheriff. "Suspect that's our cue to head back to the house."

Joe nodded. "Uh-huh. We'll get the third degree like Myron was giving those rednecks if we don't...Vertis knows what goes on in these clubs."

JAMISON HOME

A gibbous moon was rising in the east as they pulled up in front of John's house.

Joe looked out the side window in the back. "Temperature's going to drop like a rock tonight with that clear sky...be colder than a well digger's ass."

John nodded. "I'd say. We best bring in some more wood for the fireplace. Keep it burning during the night...Better get the one in ya'll's bedroom fired up too."

"Good point."

"Coming in for a cup of coffee, Myron?"

"Oh, I'd like to, but been a long day. Think my tired's hanging out."

"Yep, I can imagine."

Joe and John got out and traipsed through the snow to the porch as the sheriff drove away.

"Glad you suggested we not actually drink any of that beer, John."

He grinned. "Yeah, Mame would smell it when we came through the gate."

Joe laughed. "So would Vertis."

§

Neither John nor Joe noticed the blue truck that stopped back at Haynesville Road where the turnoff to the Jamison property was.

§§§

CHAPTER TEN

JAMISON HOME

The first golden rays of old man sun were peekin' into our bedroom window, but we were already awake on account of Rosco, grandma an' grandpa's big red rooster.

I looked outside an' it was clear an' bright, what with the light reflectin' off all that snow.

UNION COUNTY

Me, Hutch, Tiny, an' Laddie were still in that deep feather bed in the bedroom 'cross the hall from the parlor an' next to mama an' daddy's room. Had four quilts on top of us—could barely move. Sure felt good 'cause it was below freezin' in there.

Tiny an' Laddie were snuggled between us under the covers, too. I got no idea how they could even breathe, but they seemed to be enjoyin' bein' under there.

We could smell bacon fryin' from the kitchen 'long with grandma's buttermilk pancakes cookin'. We had put our clothes under the quilts at the foot of the bed. There was plenty of room 'cause me an' Hutch weren't tall enough yet for our feet to reach the end.

I nudged him an' we jumped out of bed, grabbed our clothes, an' ran across the dog run hall to the parlor which also had grandpa an' grandma's bed in it—it was a big room.

Tiny an' Laddie were right on our heels. Don't much think they really wanted to get up yet, but where we went, they wanted to go.

The fire was blazin' like we figured so we stood holdin' our duds out 'tween us an' it to warm 'em up a mite. Our fronts were burnin' up an' our hineys were freezin'.

After a couple of minutes, we turned around to warm our backsides while we slipped on our overalls an' sweatshirts over our longjohns—ahhh, they were nice an' toasty.

We grabbed our coats an' watch caps after we put our boots on 'cause we knew we had to take Tiny an' Laddie out to do their thing.

"Come on kids...outside? Wanta go outside?"

Tiny was dancin' on her front paws an' Laddie started copyin' her. We opened the door again to the hallway, then the front door. Gollybum it was cold an' still as a cemetery at night—wadn't a breath stirin'.

"Gol-uh-olee!" Hutch blew his breath out in a big cloud of fog.

UNION COUNTY

Tiny an' Laddie slipped a little goin' down the steps from the stoop, figured we best scrape 'em off after breakfast. They didn't get very far out in the snow before they both squatted. Steam rose up from their backsides as they got rid of their mornin's water, makin' more of that yella snow.

Me an' Hutch looked at each other an' had the same idea—we best do likewise. We trudged over to the corner of the house an' took care of our business. Funny how the cold makes your ding-a-ling draw up—took a minute to find it. We giggled as we wrote our names in the snow—didn't take too long.

Tiny an' Laddie were already standin' at the door ready to go back inside when we got back to the steps.

We stomped the snow off our boots, opened the door, took our hats an' coats off, an' hung 'em up. Then we ran down the hall to grandma's warm kitchen.

Grandma looked over from her wood stove where she was turnin' the bacon in a cast iron skillet when we came in. "Well, look who's up...You boys about ready for breakfast?"

We both nodded an' pulled out chairs from the big round kitchen table. Daddy an' grandpa were sittin' havin' coffee. 'Spect they'd already been out milkin' Sally, feedin' Ted an' the chickens, an' gatherin' the eggs 'fore they froze when the hens got off their nests to eat the scratch scattered about on the ground.

Daddy liked doin' that here 'cause he grew up doin' it on his mama's farm in Navarro County, Texas. His daddy, my other grandpa, was killed by one of his share croppers on the place when daddy was just eight. He was standin' right beside grandpa an' said the man that shot him was drunk. Daddy was the oldest boy an' had a lot of chores to do.

Daddy had three older sisters, my aunts, Purlye, Betty Mae, an' Lollie, she's my favorite cousin, Frances Ann's mama. Fran, I call her Red, 'cause of her hair, came to visit us last summer. Daddy also had two younger sisters, Aunt Bill, really her name was Willie Lynette, but everbody called her Bill, an' then Aunt Nell—Frances Nell. An' he had two younger brothers, John Francis, I called him Unka Frank, though, and Unka Guss, it was Guss Dunn. He was a Church of Christ preacher. 'Course daddy's name was really Robert Reese, but everbody called him, Joe—that's a whole 'nother story.

Mama set a cup of hot cocoa in front of us, then my older brother, Bobby, came staggerin' in, 'bout half awake, an' he sat down. Mama brought him a cup, too. Hope he's awake enough not to spill it down his front. Sometimes his lip has a hole in it early of a mornin'.

There was already a big platter of bacon an' tube sausage on the table, with more comin', an' another platter stacked high with pancakes. Grandma set a pitchur of warmed sorghum syrup next to the pancakes 'long with a bowl of fresh churned butter.

Everthing smelled so good my mouth was waterin'—know Hutch's was too. 'Course Tiny an' Laddie were sittin' at our feet waitin' for their share.

Can't think of anything more enjoyable than sittin' in grandma's warm kitchen on a cold winter mornin' fixin' to dive into a ginormous stack of flapjacks with butter an' hot syrup, an' a rasher of home-cured bacon 'long with sausage. Wonder what the city folks are doin'?

I looked 'cross the table. "Daddy, did ya'll find out anything 'bout those killin's at that honky tonk last night?"

Mama's head snapped my way. "Henry Lightfoot, where'd you hear about honky tonks?"

"Well, the sheriff said he'd seen a blue pickup like Hutch was talkin' 'bout outside a juke joint an' I figured a juke joint was the same as in that song we heard on the radio in the car on the way down here."

She looked at me. "What song?"

UNION COUNTY

"That Hank Williams song...*Honky Tonkin'*. You know, him an' his baby'll *go honky tonkin' round this town.*" I sang that last part like I was Hank Williams.

"Hey, Foot, that ain't half bad you oughta be on the stage...think there's one leavin' in 'bout an hour." Hutch giggled.

I whacked his shoulder. "Least I know the words. You can't carry a tune in a bushel basket."

"Can too."

"Can not."

"Can too."

"Can not."

"All right, boys, that's enough." Grandma looked at grandpa. "What *did* happen last night, John? You an' Joe didn't say anything when you came in." Her sky blue eyes burned a hole through grandpa.

Grandpa an' daddy kinda looked at each other. I could hear grandpa swallow.

"Well, Mame...you see, it's like this..."

"John L. Franklin, you're messin' around."

Grandpa blushed a little an' nodded. "Yes, dear. We...uh, that is, Joe an' I got in a little disagreement with those two boys that drove that blue pickup and..."

"Ya'll got in a fight, didn't you?"

He an' daddy exchanged glances again. "Uh...yes, ma'am."

Mama looked at daddy. "Is that where that bruise on your side came from?"

"Uh...one of 'em happened to get in a lick from my blind side..."

"But Joe took care of him in short order...put him right on the floor." Grandpa grinned and bobbed his head once like Walter Brennan did to John Wayne in *Red River* when he would tell him somethin'. "And he was quite a bit bigger than Joe, too."

"And then the sheriff came in before things got too out of hand. See, he'd sent us in first so it wouldn't look like he was bringin' a big crowd in..."

Grandpa nodded at daddy. "That's right. He thought it might keep him from getting any information..."

Daddy looked at mama, then grandma. "Turns out it worked out for the best because he had to shoot a broken table leg out of one of those redneck's hand..."

Mama's mouth dropped open. "Had to what?"

Daddy held up his hands in front of him to mama. "Uh, Vertis, honey, he came in, just as planned, and it happened to be when one of those fellas with the blue truck had picked up a table leg..."

Grandma turned to grandpa. "How did a table get broken?"

Daddy continued with the story. It was great. I was really enjoyin' this.

"John picked up this little fella that was pestering him whaling away at his stomach, and threw him halfway across the room where he landed on this table and..."

Grandpa was 6'3 an' weighed 'bout 285, that's why they call him Big John.

Grandma slapped her dishtowel on the table. "Enough! We've heard enough.

These boys don't need to be hearing all this."

"It's awright Grandma. This is better'n the movies. Like a Big Boy Williams an' Johnny Mack Brown fight scene in a old west saloon or somethin'." I looked at Hutch. "Ain't that right?"

His eyes were big as saucers as he nodded. "Uh-huh."

She rolled her eyes at the ceilin'. "Oh, my Lord in Heaven."

Then she turned to grandpa. "We'll talk more later, mister."

"Yes, dear." He picked up his saucered an' blowed coffee to hide his face an' took a long sip.

Mama looked just like grandma when she bumped daddy's arm. "You, too...Now eat your breakfast."

Daddy did his little grin an' winked at her. That always gets mama.

"Yes, dear."

I had a smile on my face big as the moon just before I took a big bite of my flapjacks drippin' with syrup. "I gotta jot all this down. Might write a story one day an' this is good stuff."

Mama just glared at me.

§§§

CHAPTER ELEVEN

JAMISON HOME

My cousins from up the road at Unka JB's, Don an' Hubert, walked the hundred yards through the snow from their house to grandma an' grandpa's. They had already done their chores an' came down to see if we wanted to go slidin' on Red Hill road.

UNION COUNTY

Me an' Hutch jumped up 'cause it sounded like fun. They had several pieces of cardboard boxes they were gonna use an' grandma had a couple she let us have. We cut 'em apart so we could use the biggest piece for a sled.

We waded through the snow to the top of Red Hill road. It was only 'bout thirty yards from the house. There hadn't been nobody drive down it, so it was still smooth. Tiny an' Laddie decided they didn't want to go on 'count it was too hard for them to get through the snow.

It was almost a hundred yards down to the bottom. Don went first. He grabbed the top of his cardboard and ran a couple of steps—hard to do in the ten inches of snow—dove forward on his belly on top of his makeshift sled. By holdin' the front edge up that cardboard slid down the hill like it was greased.

I went next. Bellied down on my cardboard an' whoo-boy, went flyin' down that hill. Was goin' so fast the wind in my eyes was makin' it hard to see till I came to an abrupt stop at the bottom when I plowed into a snow bank.

Dug myself out, laughin' all the while. Don was laughin' 'long with me.

"You completely disappeared, Foot. Couldn't see nothin' but your feet. Same thing happened to me." He pointed past the pile of snow. "Good thing that was there...we'd of run smooth into those pine trees."

"Dang! That woulda left a mark."

"Ya think?"

We'd no more than got out of the way when Hubert plowed into the bank. He laid there a minute just kickin' his feet till it dawned on us he couldn't get out. Me an Don grabbed a foot each an' pulled him backwards so he could stand up.

He turned around an' dug the snow from his eyes. "Hey, thanks guys, couldn't breathe there for a second...Look out!"

We jumped to the side as Hutch careened into the bank. Instead of stoppin' like us, he shot over it like a ski jump, went between two big pine trees an' finally came to a stop in a briar patch.

"Oh, Lordy, ya'll help me!"

Me an' Don ran up to him.

I looked down. "What are you tryin' to do, play-like Brer Rabbit?"

I reached out to grab his hand. Don took the other one.

"I'd say he looks more like Tar Baby to me."

We got him pulled up out of the briars an' he whacked Don a good one on his shoulder. Don just giggled 'cause he had enough clothes on it didn't hurt any.

We gathered up our cardboard sleds an' I looked at everbody, then up the hill. "We got a problem, guys."

Hutch frowned. "What kinda problem?"

I pointed. "We gotta climb that hill."

Don stopped gigglin'. "Shoot, forgot about that part."

Thirty minutes later when we got to the top, Don turned to the rest of us. "Don't know 'bout ya'll, but think I've enjoyed 'bout all the sleddin' I can handle."

Hutch nodded. "Uh-huh, that climb up the hill 'bout did me in...Don't think I want to do it again."

"Let's go see if grandma'll make us some hot cocoa or hot milk."

Hubert poked me. "Way to go, Foot. Usin' your head for something 'sides a hat rack."

I poked him back. "Well, knew none of ya'll would think of it."

He stuck his tongue out at me, so I picked up a handful of snow an' chunked it at him. That started it—the snowball fight was on.

We kept throwin' at each other till we saw the sheriff's Ford pull up in front of the house.

"Hey, Hutch, let's go an' see if the sheriff has anymore news on the killer."

"Yeah, or killers."

Hubert stood up. "What killers?"

Don hit him with one more snowball right in the forehead, knockin' him back on his butt.

He rolled over an' got back up rubbin' his head. "Dang you, Don, that wadn't fair, I wadn't lookin'. You just wait."

"All's fair in love an' snowball fights, little brother."

"Yeah, well, you'll find out when you least expect it."

"Oooh, I'm scared."

"Just wait...you'll be sorry."

Me an' Hutch didn't hear no more as we hot footed it to the house as Sheriff Wilson was goin' in the front door.

Took us a few minutes on the porch to stomp the snow off our boots an' brush it from our coats 'fore we could go inside. Grandma'll have our hides if we track all that in her house.

We shucked our coats an' hats an' hung 'em up, then headed to the kitchen to warm up.

Sheriff Wilson was already sittin' at the table an' grandma had just set a mug of steamin' coffee in front of him when we walked in.

She looked up at our cheeks an' noses that were rosy from the cold. "You boys look like you could use some hot milk."

We all nodded an' took chairs at the table. It was close enough to her stove we could feel the heat—sure felt good. Think the coldest thing 'bout us was our hands an' feet. Wouldn't take long to thaw up in the kitchen, though. Love grandma' hot milk. It's like melted vanilla ice cream.

We decided best be quiet on account the sheriff was talkin' to grandpa an' daddy.

He kinda pinched his lips together an' shook his head 'fore he started the tellin'.

"Same thing...Bashed old man Krause's head in...killed his dog, too. Place was ransacked, especially his bookcase."

Grandpa looked at daddy, then at the sheriff. "His house is within a half-mile of Haynesville Road, too, isn't it?"

"It is." He blew across the top of his cup, took a sip, then looked back up. "Whoever it was had chains on...Impossible to tell if it was a car or pickup, though."

"Any pages missin' from his Bible?"

The sheriff shook his head. "Didn't look like it, Joe."

Grandma looked over from the stove where she was stirrin' our hot milk. "Did you say Krause, Myron? That's Earnest Krause?"

"That's right, Mame, why?"

"Isn't he or should I say, wasn't he supposed to be related to Bonnie Parker?...Cousin of her mama or something?"

Grandpa nodded. "By golly, Mame, believe you're right. Told me one time over at Jolley's Store he knew Bonnie well and they were fairly close...Think he said second cousins...was about twenty years older than her." He chuckled. "Said as a child, she was kind of head strong."

When grandpa was done, the sheriff added, "Apparently didn't change much, then."

I looked at Hutch, then at the sheriff. "Wadn't she some kind of bank robber back a long time ago?"

"About twenty years...How'd you know about that, Foot?"

I shrugged. "Had a thing 'bout her an' her boyfriend Clyde's car all shot to pieces by the po-lice down in Louisiana on one of those Warner Pathe News reels at the pitchur show up in Colorado."

"Really?"

"Uh-huh. Was showing that shot up V-8 Ford at some fairs...musta had a jillion holes in it. An' one of the cops, a former Texas Ranger, Frank Hamer, was upset 'bout 'em showin' it. Tol' the guy doin' it he had to quit. Not sure why."

"Yeah, met Frank once when he was still a Texas Ranger...one tough hombre. Story has it that he killed over forty men...and one woman, Bonnie Parker, in his tenure as a lawman. Said he wasn't proud of killin' a woman, but had to be done. There was no way they were going to be taken alive."

"Gol-uh-olee." Hutch's mouth dropped open.

I elbowed him an' he closed it.

Grandpa cocked his head. "Weren't they comin' from Missouri or somewhere?"

The sheriff shook his head. "Believe it was Shreveport."

"Reckon they could have swung through Union County on the way, to see her cousin...good old Earnest?"

The sheriff scratched the side of his face. "Entirely possible, John. The ambush was near Sailes, in Bienville Parrish, just fifty miles or so south of here."

Grandma poured up the four mugs of hot milk an' set 'em on the table in front of us. "Do you think they would have stopped just for a visit? That doesn't really make a lot of sense for outlaws on the run."

I took of sip from my cup. "Maybe they left something with her cousin...bank money or somethin'?"

The sheriff looked over at me. "You know, Foot, now, that's not too far fetched...for a country boy." He grinned. "They didn't find any money to speak of in their car after the ambush."

"None of their bank loot was ever recovered from what I know. Used to hear 'em talk about Clyde down home back in Texas. He was born in Telico, just a few miles from Dawson, where I was born. I was a young man, rough-neckin' in the oil patch around there when they were on their robbin' spree."

The sheriff looked at daddy. "Ever hear of Clyde coming back to visit the home place when you were there?"

"Every once in a while. The locals looked on him and Bonnie as kind of Robin Hoods...born of the depression."

Grandpa leaned back in his chair. "Well, if I've said it once, I've said it a hundred times...don't believe in coincidences. If Bonnie and Clyde came through here...they had a reason."

The sheriff nodded. "I agree, John...and other than just to visit kin, too."

§§§

CHAPTER TWELVE

SALEM ROAD

Sheriff Wilson stopped his black Ford county vehicle in front of Earnest Krause's house as the ambulance attendants, Pete and Charlie, were leavin' with the body to take it to Doc Duckworth on account he's the coroner for Union County. We all waved at one another.

UNION COUNTY

The sheriff, grandpa, daddy, an' us got out of the car and walked through the snow to the front door. It was fairly easy 'cause of all the previous tracks. Me an' Hutch were right on their heels.

I leaned over to him. "Can't believe the sheriff let us come."

He nodded. "Guess he's noticed how interested we were."

"Uh-huh. Could be."

"Sun's meltin' the snow. Keeps this up it'll be gone by late tomorrow."

Joe grinned. "Just like Texas, John...Snow one day at twenty degrees or less and it's seventy in two days...Little different in Colorado, though. Gets cold up there and stays that way for a while...They even flood the city park in Fort Morgan, where we live, at the first cold snap for ice skating. Stays frozen most of the winter."

Sheriff looked over his shoulder as he stepped up on the porch. "Boys, don't touch anything until you ask my permission, okay? We're going to try to collect evidence...finger prints an' the like."

"Yessir...we just wanna watch." I glanced at Hutch. "Ain't that so?"

"Uh-huh."

Noticed Sheriff Wilson was carryin' some kinda kit. Looked sorta like a high dollar tackle box—but bet it wadn't.

We went inside an' it was no warmer than outside. Reckon the sheriff musta turned the space heater off when he was here before. No need in keepin' it goin—now.

He set that tackle box lookin' kit on the coffee table, opened it, took out some white rubber doctor gloves, put 'em on, then got a kinda puffer thing. After squeezin' it 'long the top edge of the bookcase, there was a fine coatin' of a black powder on the varnish.

I turned to Hutch. "That's called graphite...sorta like ground up pencil lead. Gonna brush it off now."

Sure 'nuff, he took a small paint brush an' lightly swept most of the powder away.

Son-of-a-gun, there were some round things left showin'.

I elbowed Hutch. "Those are finger prints."

"I know...Not stupid."

I shrugged. "Just didn't know you got that far yet."

"Talked 'bout 'em in that Sherlock Holmes book I read."

"Oh, right."

The sheriff took a roll of see-through tape from his kit—think they call it Scotch tape, don't know why, it's not from Scotland. He pressed it on those prints that were showin', then lifted it up, takin' the rest of that black powder with it. Then he stuck the tape on a white card an' there those fingerprints were, just like on the bookcase. Guess he'll take the card to his office an' look at 'em with a magnafyin' glass.

If he arrests some guy with the same prints—then he's probably the one that did the killin'. Love seein' this stuff like in the books.

"That Holmes book said wadn't no two fingerprints alike."

I looked at Hutch an' frowned. "Yeah, I know."

"Huh...Thought you mighta missed that part."

I whacked him—he whacked me back.

"Not hardly...ding dong."

"You're the ding dong."

"No, you are."

"Uh-uh, you are..."

Daddy looked over at us with his special *shut up* look. We both drew our fingers across our lips. Those brown eyes of his can cut a hole right through you—doesn't need words.

Hutch elbowed me. "How come you got blue eyes an' your daddy has brown?"

"I don't know...took after mama an' grandpa, I guess."

Daddy an' grandpa were eyeballin' everthing in the room, specially the cut up couch an' chairs.

"They sure must of thought Krause had something hidden in here. You might be right about Bonnie and Clyde leaving something, John."

"Kind of looking that way, Joe. Cut these couch cushions and pillows all to pieces." He lifted a couple of them up. "Don't think there was anything here, though."

Sheriff Wilson squatted on the floor an' was studyin' the open Bible. "Think I was wrong."

Grandpa looked over at him. "About what, Myron?"

"The family page is gone after all. Didn't leave a rough edge like over at the last place."

"Can you get any fingerprints from the Bible, Sheriff?"

"No, Foot, the cover is a pebbly kind of leather...too rough to hold a print...Good thought, though."

"Did they look behind the bookcase?" I pointed at it.

He looked over at me with one eyebrow raised.

I shrugged. "They hid somethin' in one of my Hardy Boys books by tapin' it to the back of a bookcase."

"They didn't look...but I will." He stood, stepped over to the case, an' pulled one side away from the wall and looked behind it.

§

A quarter of a mile further down Salem Road, two sets of eyes watched the Krause house from their vehicle parked at the edge of a curve.

"They sure been in there a while...Wonder what they're doin'?"

"The sheriff's doin' his job an' investigatin' a crime...He ain't gonna find nothin', though."

"Wouldn't be too sure, we didn't have enough time to look everywhere."

"We looked good enough. Need to follow those names. The boss wants a list."

§

"Well, I'll be darned." The sheriff reached back behind the bookcase an' pulled out a folded piece of paper with some adhesive tape I could tell used to be white across it. "Wonder what we have here?"

"Looks like it's been there a while, Myron."

"Does, doesn't it, John?"

He was real careful as he unfolded the yellowed paper after layin' it on the coffee table. The tape was still on it. Guess he figured it might tear the paper if he tried to remove it or somethin'—looked pretty dry.

Me an' Hutch crowded up close as we could without gettin' in daddy an' grandpa's way. That would have been a mistake.

"Looks like some kind of map. Can't make heads nor tails of it, though."

Daddy pointed at some writin'. "Wonder what that means, Myron?"

He was pointin' at a word. The only one on the piece of paper—*Cookie.*

The sheriff shook his head. "Got no idea, Joe...No idea at all. Makes no sense to me." He looked at grandpa. "John?"

Both his eyebrows went up. "Me either, Myron...That's a real mystery."

Daddy nodded. "This whole thing's a real mystery."

JAMISON HOME

Tiny an' Laddie were waitin' for us on the porch. They were layin' down at the end where the sun was shinin'. Soakin' up some rays, I 'magine.

Grandpa, daddy, an' us got out of the sheriff's car.

"Thanks for goin' with me." He looked at me an' Hutch. "And especially you boys. Would have never thought to look behind that bookcase...Now, just to figure out what it means."

Grandpa shook his head. "Lots of luck on that, Myron."

UNION COUNTY

I had taken my Big Chief tablet with me an' sketched a copy of it on one page. Me an' Hutch would work on it some.

"Boys, I gotta run to the feed store. Need grain and hay for Sally and Ted and chicken scratch for Rosco and his girls...ya'll want to come?"

We nodded. "Yeah, Grandpa, love goin' to Mister Wortham's."

"Comin' Joe?"

Daddy grinned. "Might as well, John, can't dance."

Now I don't know what dancin's got to do with goin' to a feed store—must be an adult thing. But after grandpa had me run inside to tell mama an' grandma. I put my tablet up while I was inside, then we all headed to his big ol' two ton International Harvester flat bed truck parked under the shed at the barn. Knew right off we weren't gonna ride on the back—still too cold.

We all got in the front seat. Hutch had to straddle the long gearshift stickin' up from the floor.

Grandpa pulled out the choke in the dash, pushed in the clutch, pumped the gas pedal a couple times, an' stepped on the starter button next to it. The big engine turned over slow at first, guess it was cold too. He pushed in the choke, then pulled it out again, an' stepped on the starter one more time.

The engine caught, ran like a three legged mule, till grandpa pushed the choke back in, then it started runnin' smooth. He let it run a bit to warm up, then shifted backwards an' to his leg into reverse, backed out, an' we headed for the feed store.

The dual rear wheel truck didn't need no chains, it had mud an' snow tires on the back—can go through most anything.

§§§

CHAPTER THIRTEEN

JUNCTION CITY, ARKANSAS

The roads were mostly free from packed snow an' ice from the sun beatin' down on 'em an' the traffic by the time we reached Wortham's Feed.

There were already some pickups parked out front an' side. One was backed up to the loadin' dock at a big wide door on the side of the buildin' an' another was backed into the hay barn out behind the store. 'Spect it's folks needin' feed for their stock like grandpa.

It would be a little bit till the guy backed up to the side was loaded, so grandpa'd have to wait.

We all got out an' stepped up on the porch where several fellas were standin' 'round doin' what grandpa called, 'chewin' the fat'.

Now, I don't know what fat has to do with visitin', but that's what it was called around here. It had warmed up considerable, that's why those men were standin' around on the porch just smokin' or chewin' tabacca. Want to give them a wide berth on account of the burstin' radius.

They all seemed to know grandpa but that's not surprisin' since the family's been in the area before bully was a pup. That's another one of his sayin's an' I got no idea in the world who or what bully is, but he's a pup.

"John, see you made it out awright."

"Did, Simon. Not much can stop old Bertha."

That's what he called his big ol' truck, like daddy calls his car 'Huldy'. Don't know what that means, either.

We went inside an' there was a potbellied stove in the middle of the room. There was some other fellas sittin' around it in straight back slat chairs—musta been chewin' the fat, too, as well as eatin' roasted peanuts.

The owner, Mister Wortham, was an' older, gray-haired man was standin' behind the counter. Looked to be 'bout the same age as grandpa. He was tall an' slender with a white mustache. Had a nice look to his eyes. Grandpa stuck out his hand when he walked up.

"Clive, good to see you."

"You, too, John...Who you got there with you?"

"This is my son-in-law, Joe Lee...Joe, meet the best feed man in the area, Clive Wortham."

He grinned as he stuck out his hand to daddy. "Only feed man in the area, actually. Where ya'll from?"

Daddy smiled back an' nodded. "Originally from Texas but right now, Fort Morgan, Colorado."

"Joe's a driller for Shell Oil. They came down to get away from the cold for his vacation."

Mister Wortham glanced at grandpa, then back to daddy. "So, you're the cause."

I looked up. "What does he mean, Daddy? Cause of what?"

"Uh, this is my son, Foot, Clive...That other young man is his friend, Hutch."

Mister Wortham chuckled from deep inside. "I mean, we didn't have all this snow till ya'll showed up an' brought it down with you."

"Sir?"

"Just funnin' you, son, just funnin' you...Foot, that's an interestin' name, bet there's a story there somewhere."

UNION COUNTY

Daddy tosseled my hair. "His name's really Henry Lightfoot Lee...They're family names from back around the American revolution. We shortened it to *Foot* when he was just a little shaver."

"You don't say?"

"That ain't near as odd as my best friend here's name, Mister Wortham." I pointed at Hutch with my thumb.

He bent over an' put his hands on the top of his wood plank counter. "How so?"

"His real name's Seymore Washington Grant, but his mama kept house for some folks in El Dorado. His grandma said they kept their fine china in a thing they called a 'Hutch', an' since she thought her baby was fine...she started callin' him *Hutch*..." I elbowed him in the side. "...Sure glad it wadn't a chifferobe."

Mister Wortham leaned back, started laughin' an' snortin'...thought he was gonna choke for a minute.

Hutch poked me back. We horse around a lot...I turned my head, closed my eyes an' took a deep breath.

I looked up. "Grandpa, how come feed stores always smell so good?...I could stay in here all day."

He looked down at me. "It's mostly the sweet feed all feed stores carry for horses. But you have to add in the alfalfa, too."

There was an' open bag of cattle cubes sittin' in front of the counter. Guess it was for customers could give it a look-see 'fore they buy it. They smelled good, too. I reached in an' got one. It was 'bout the size of daddy's thumb.

I took a bite off one end an' chewed it up.

Mister Wortham laughed again. "Never seen a boy come in here they didn't grab a cattle cube an' eat on it...come to think of it, do it myself on occasion...Good, aren't they, Foot?"

I looked up at him an' nodded. "Yessir."

Hutch reached in an' grabbed him one, too.

Mister Wortham nodded again. "It's that an' lickin' on a salt block...never fails."

"Speakin' of, Clive, need a couple hundred pounds of sweet feed an' a hundred pounds of whole oats for Ted, my mule."

Mister Wortham opened up a pad an' went to writin' down what grandpa was orderin'. He nodded an' looked back up ready for more, I reckon.

"Guess you can add a couple hundred pounds of those cattle cubes, for Sally...along with a mineral salt block, five bales of orchard grass hay, an' ten bales of alfalfa...When your boys finish loadin' Peavy's truck."

"We can get that. Won't be but a couple more minutes...Heard you're back helpin' the sheriff some."

Grandpa nodded. "Occasionally."

"Any news on the killin's?"

Grandpa frowned an' kinda pressed his lips together. "Afraid so, Clive. Earnest

Krause was found murdered this mornin'."

He shook his head. "Ernie? Damnation, that's a shame. He was in a few days ago. Just before the storm hit...Same killer?"

"Looked to be so. Sheriff an' I gave the scene a goin' over before he dropped us off at the house so I could get my truck. He took some evidence to town for analysis."

"What kind of evidence?"

Grandpa glanced around the front of the store. "Not really at liberty to say, at this time."

"Understand...Hope ya'll catch whoever's doin' it 'fore anybody else gets hurt."

"Tryin', Clive, we're tryin'...Just tryin' to figure out the why of it."

I glanced over an' noticed some of the fellas over at the stove were tryin' to listen in. Don't know who they were, though.

"Any leads?"

Grandpa nodded. "Well, maybe...How long you been here in the area, Clive?."

He looked up at the ceilin' for a second. "Moved here from Dallas in '29...when the depression hit. Why?"

"Just wondered how well you knew, Ernie."

"Well, we used to hunt an' fish together back when we were younger...Guess you could say I knew him better'n most."

"He ever say anything about his kinfolks?"

"Come to think of it, said at one time he was related to Bonnie Parker...cousin or somethin'. Used to kinda brag 'bout it." He stopped to think a minute. "Fact is, was kinda upset for a while when she an' Clyde were killed not far south of here in Louisiana in '34...Never was too sure but what he didn't have more'n one noose in his family tree his own self."

"What about any relatives here local?"

Mister Wortham scratched the side of his face, thought again, an' finally shook his head. "Seems like it, John, but can't remember...Slept once or twice since then." He glanced over his shoulder.

"Looks like the boys got ol' Peavy loaded...you can pull your truck in now for the feed, then we'll go over to the hay barn."

One of those fellas that were sittin' around the stove got up an' hurried out the front door.

I turned to Hutch. "Wonder why that man was all of a sudden in a hurry. He's just been sittin' there eatin' peanuts from that wood nail keg since we came in, now he's out the door like he forgot somethin'."

"Maybe he had to go pee."

I shook my head. "Outhouse is in back, next to the hay barn."

I could see out the front window an' watched as the man got in his pickup an' drove off—still had a hurry on.

§§§

CHAPTER FOURTEEN

JAMISON HOME

"What'd that fella look like you saw hurry off while we were at the feed store, Foot?" Grandpa was backin' into the barn to unload the feed an' hay.

I looked up at him from my place between daddy an' Hutch. "Younger'n daddy, had brown hair stickin' out from underneath a beat-up gray hat an' wore khaki pants like a lots of men do...Got in a dark green Ford pickup. Couldn't tell what year it was...all purty much look the same since the war."

Hutch elbowed me. "Was wearin' a canvas coat, too."

"Yeah, right...that too."

"Have a mustache or beard?"

"No, sir. Needed a shave, though."

"Why didn't you tell me then?"

"Cause you were already headed out to pull your truck up to the dock when he jumped up an' run off."

Grandpa looked over at daddy. "You see anything, Joe?"

"Not so much, John. Saw those fellas sitting around the stove eatin' peanuts, but didn't pay 'em much mind."

"Yeah, me too."

"See which way he went, Foot?"

"Yessir, back toward the Haynesville Road...Couldn't tell which way from there."

"Joe, why don't you run over to Jolley's Store an' call that in to the sheriff while I unload this stuff."

"Sure you don't want me to help?"

"Naw, no hill for a stepper...Be done an' in the house by the time ya'll get back."

"Okay, let's go, boys."

We went out, got in daddy's 1950 Ford sedan an' drove the short distance over to the store—it was on Haynesville Road. Daddy parked in front an' we all got out an' went inside. Most of the snow was gone from the gravel parkin' lot.

Mister Jolley didn't have a potbellied stove like at the feed store, but he did have a space heater that had the ceramic things in the front just a glowin'. It was nice an' warm in there, almost hot, but the day had heated up some, too.

"Come in, Joe, what can I do for you?"

"Need to use the phone, Smead, if that's all right,?"

"Sure go right ahead." He reached in a jar on his counter an' grabbed a couple of penny candies. "Here you go, boys, put these in your pockets. Know it's too close to supper time. Mame an' Vertis will come over to peel my head if you eat 'em now."

We both thanked him an' grinned while we put the red jaw breakers in our pockets for later.

"Thanks, Mister Jolley."

"Uh-huh...I'll tell Mame you'll be out for supper, Myron. See you in a bit." Daddy hung the phone back on the receiver at the wall.

"See you've learned about sayin' too much on that party line, Joe."

Daddy smiled. "Yeah, we have party lines up at home, too, Smead. Need to be careful when givin' messages to the sheriff...Not much difference, I would imagine." He looked at me an' Hutch. "You boys ready?"

We had walked over to the comic book rack while daddy finished with the sheriff. "Yessir."

"See anything you like?"

I shook my head. "Uh-uh, already got the ones I read regular."

"Thought as much."

We turned an' headed to the front door.

Daddy waved over his shoulder. "Thanks again, Smead."

"Anytime."

HAYNESVILLE ROAD

Two vehicles were parked one behind the other. The man from the green pickup that had left Wortham's Feed store earlier leaned into the passenger window of the vehicle in front.

"That's what Jamison told Wortham."

"What else?"

"Wortham said he used to hunt an' fish with Krause back when they were younger..."

"And?"

"Well, then they talked a bit 'bout old man Krause bein' related to Bonnie Parker."

The two men inside looked at each other.

"Jamison asked Wortham if Krause ever talked about any other relatives local."

"Did he?"

"Said he thought so...but couldn't remember who right off."

The two men looked at one another again, both nodded and watched a light green 1950 Ford sedan with a sun visor over the front windshield pull away from Jolley's Store up the road a ways.

"All right, good work. Keep your eyes an' ears open."

The man walked back to his pickup, got in, made a U turn, and drove away.

"Sounds like they may know something."

"Yeah...That could be trouble."

UNION COUNTY

JAMISON HOME

Daddy pulled up in front of the house. Tiny an' Laddie were on the porch watchin' us get out. An' true to his word, grandpa was sittin' out there, too, in his rocker, with a cup of coffee in his hand.

"Could you tell what kind of vehicles were parked down the road, Foot?"

I shook my head. "No, sir. Settin' sun was in my eyes. Just could tell there was two of 'em 'bout half-mile toward El Dorado at the edge of that curve."

"I couldn't see nothin' neither," added Hutch.

Tiny an' Laddie met us on the walk up to the porch, just a wigglin' an' dancin' around our legs. They were both glad to see us.

Me an' Hutch sat down on the edge of the porch, so we could pet on Tiny an' the puppy while daddy an' grandpa talked.

"Myron said he'd be right out...speaking of, guess I'd better go tell Mame to set another plate."

Grandpa chuckled. "No need. When I told her you drove over to Smead's with the boys to call him, she automatically set another place at the table...Knows him too well."

"Ah, yeah, didn't think about that."

Twenty minutes later, Sheriff Wilson pulled up out front an' parked. He got out, came through the gate, an' headed to the porch. Tiny an' Laddie ran out to meet him on the walkway.

"Well, hello, Tiny, and who is your friend?" He squatted down to pet on 'em.

"His name's Laddie, Sheriff. He showed up durin' the snow storm an' guess I adopted...or he adopted me."

The sheriff looked at Hutch as he climbed the steps. "Looks like he's mostly border collie...good dogs."

"Yessir, that's what Mister John said. Also said they were real smart."

"So I've heard, Hutch. So I've heard." He turned to daddy. "Now, what was that information you called about, Joe?"

Daddy looked at me an' Hutch. "Tell the sheriff what ya'll saw, Foot."

"Yessir...We were over to Mister Wortham's Feed. Grandpa had to get some stuff. An' while we were there, me an' Hutch saw a guy sittin' over by the stove eatin' on the peanuts payin' a whole lots of attention to grandpa an' Mister Wortham while they were talkin' 'bout that Mister Krause man an' his kin..."

"His kin?"

"Uh-huh...'Cause him an' Mister Wortham used to go fishin' an' huntin' together...Grandpa asked if that Parker lady bank robber that got killed by the po-lice down in Louisiana had any more kin around here 'sides Mister Krause."

"Oh, right...Go on."

"Mister Wortham said he thought so, but had slept since then an' couldn't remember...but he'd think on it."

I looked at Hutch to pick it up there.

"When Mister John went to pull his truck up to the loadin' dock for the feed, that fella jumped up, ran an' got in his pickup an' took off like a pack of dogs were after him."

The sheriff took out a little notepad thing from his pocket an' made a couple of notes. He looked back up. "Can you boys tell me what he looked like?"

We looked at each other again an' Hutch nodded to me.

"Yessir, some. He wadn't quite old as daddy."

"Thanks a lot, Foot."

I grinned. "You know what I mean, Daddy...you ain't old. He was just younger'n you."

He nodded an' smiled back.

"The man had brown hair...kinda long...stickin' out from underneath a dirty gray hat like daddy's..."

"Fedora, Foot."

"Yessir, that kind. Was wearin' a red an' black plaid shirt an' khakis." I glanced at Hutch.

"An' a canvas jacket. He jumped in a dark green Ford pickup an' tore out of Mister Wortham's lot."

"All right, that helps a lot, boys." He put his pad back in his shirt pocket.

Grandpa, daddy, an' the sheriff, turned to go inside when a fella I never seen before drove up real fast in an old Dodge pickup, stopped out front an' ran up to the porch—he was all out of breath.

"Sheriff Wilson! Sheriff, sure glad I caught you here. You gotta come."

"Whoa, calm down...What is it, Murf?"

"It's Clive Wortham...Somebody has beat him to death!"

§§§

CHAPTER FIFTEEN

JAMISON HOME

"Mame, keep our dinner warm, we have to go back over to the feed store..."

"What is it, John?" Grandma dried her hands on a dish towel.

Grandpa frowned. "Murf Poole just came by to tell the sheriff Clive Wortham's been murdered down at his store."

Grandma an' mama both put their hands to their mouths.

"Oh, John...no! My God in Heaven, what's going on around here?" She looked at mama. "We'll have to fix some food for Mariam tomorrow and take it over."

"How long had they been married?"

"Almost fifty years."

Mama shook her head. "Such a pity. Know she'll be devastated."

Grandma looked back at grandpa. "Was it a robbery?"

He shook his head, then mashed his lips together before he said anything.

"Don't think so...but we'll find out. Be back when we're done."

"Can we go, Grandpa?"

He put his thick hand on my shoulder. "No, Foot, you an' Hutch need to stay here. The sheriff, your daddy, and I will tell you all about it when we get back...We don't know what we're going to find. Probably won't be too pretty."

Me an' Hutch glanced at each other. Think he was almost as disappointed as me.

WORTHAM'S FEED

Sheriff Wilson pulled up in front of the shiplap sided store in need of a paint job and stopped. The county ambulance, from El Dorado, was already there.

The regular attendants, Pete and Charlie, in their white hospital uniforms, were leaning against the front of their World War II surplus field ambulance, smoking cigarettes, waiting on the sheriff to get there.

"Made good time, Pete." The sheriff stepped out of his car as Joe handed him the kit from the back seat he used on crime scenes.

"Yessir, Deputy Walker called us straight away, right after Murf called your office lookin' for you."

"Murf caught me at John's. Anybody been inside?"

"No, sir...Least not since we got here. Know how you are 'bout that. We kept everybody out." He glanced over at the several pickups parked to the side.

The drivers and passengers were outside of them watching what was going on.

"Good thinkin'. Far as I know, Murf was the only one that looked inside. Said he saw Clive's truck still parked next to the store after closin' time. Came inside to check and found the poor devil." He handed Joe and John a pair of white surgical gloves as they walked toward the door.

Doctor Duckworth, a local doctor who doubled as the County Coroner, stopped his Buick next to the ambulance before they reached the porch.

"Well, glad you finally made it, you old quack. Thought I was going to have to check the body without you."

He laughed. "That would have been a joke, you wouldn't have a clue what you were lookin' at...Damn tin star toter."

The sheriff grabbed the door knob and pushed the front door open. "I'll tin star you...You probably got your medical degree through the mail from a catalogue."

"Better'n a Cracker Jack box like your badge."

John grinned and leaned over to Joe as Doctor Duckworth followed the sheriff inside. "You'd think those two hated each other's guts. Truth is, they've been best friends since grade school...Talk to each other that way since I've known 'em."

Joe nodded. "Yeah...Got a friend on my crew. We do the same thing. Been with me for ten years...He's my derrick man."

"Whoa, look at this."

They looked around at the devastation as they stepped inside. Aisle counters overturned, cans of oil scattered around, bags of seed corn broken open, corn everywhere. Cattle and horse medicine bottles scattered about. Even the main counter with the cash register was turned over.

"Old war horse must have put up a hellova fight. Had to have been at least two...Maybe three. One man's not going to take Clive Wortham down."

Joe picked up a pocket that had been torn from a red plaid shirt. "Looks familiar."

"Lord, Lord...Used some kind of club on him, too. Broken forearm...defensive, skint and bruised knuckles on both hands. I'd say he gave almost as good as he got." The doctor palpated the back of Wortham's head. "Massive concussion. That's what killed him...One of them hit him from behind with something."

The sheriff shook his head. "Bastards."

"I'm going to say three men did this, Myron...He was hit from all sides." Doctor Duckworth checked his ribs. "Kicked him after he was down, too...broken ribs."

"Joe, check the cash register on the floor over there."

"Never opened it, looks like, Myron."

"He still has his billfold." The doctor held it up. "Full of cash."

The sheriff shook his head. "Not robbery...Being vindicatory for some reason." He looked over at John and Joe. "Making sure he kept his mouth shut."

"That he didn't remember anything about Krause's local kin." John glanced back at the sheriff and nodded.

Joe held up the scrap of cloth.

John nodded. "Now we just have to find out who that was that overheard my conversation with Clive."

"The one the boys saw leave in a hurry?...Did you know any of those others sittin' with him around the stove, John?...There was three of them beside the guy in the plaid shirt and khaki pants."

"Could be, Joe, could be."

The sheriff turned to John. "Well, don't keep me in the dark."

UNION COUNTY

HAYNESVILLE ROAD

Jimmy Jack and Billy watched the sheriff drive off with John and Joe as they sat parked back up the Haynesville Road.

Billy glanced over at his friend. "Looks like they're gone, Jimmy Jack, now's our chanct."

Jimmy Jack put his blue '47 Chevy pickup in gear and pulled out on the road.

JAMISON HOME

Me and Hutch were playin' cars with our stuff out in the front of the house—buildin' roads an' ramps in the soft, wet sand. Bobby had gone down to Don an' Hubert's. We looked up as a blue truck stopped by the trees.

"Foot, that's the truck I seen over to Miz Riggs road...an' them same two red necks."

Tiny an' Laddie ran to the gate barkin' a warnin'. Well, Laddie wadn't doin' much more than a yip or two.

"Tiny, get back here. Come on."

She turned an' looked at me, not sure she should.

"Come on." I patted my leg an' she an' Laddie trotted back to us, glancin' over their shoulders at the two men.

They came through the gate, left it open, an' walked up toward where we were playin'.

"What do ya'll want here?" I stood up, then Hutch stood up beside me.

"Oh, we just come by to deliver a message to that big old man an' his son-in-law." The man talkin' looked at his friend. "Ain't that so, Billy."

"Yep, Jimmy Jack, right as rain. That's why we're here, awright...to deliver a message."

"That'd be my grandpa an' my daddy."

"You don't say?"

UNION COUNTY

I looked at the one named Jimmy Jack right in the eye, like daddy always taught me to do. "Just did."

"You're a bit of a little smart ass, ain'tcha, boy?" said the one called Billy.

"Just speakin' the truth, mister...like my daddy tells me to always do."

"What kind of message you come to deliver?"

Jimmy Jack looked down at Hutch, then back at me. "Who's the nigger?"

"He's my best friend, that's who...an' I don't much like that word."

Jimmy Jack bent over, grabbed the front of my jacket an' pulled me closer. "I don't really care what you like or don't like, kid. He's black as three feet up a bull's butt an' that makes him a nigger to me."

I kicked him in the shin with my winter lace-up boots. Had to hurt like the dickens.

He turned loose of my jacket an' grabbed his leg, an' then I hauled off an' hit him hard as I could right on his nose.

His eyes bugged out as he staggered backward a couple of steps an' dropped to his hiney. Blood was just a pourin' out of both nostrils down his face.

The one he called Billy just stood there with his mouth hangin' open lookin' down at Jimmy Jack. "What're you doin'?"

Hutch saw his chance, grabbed the front of Billy's coat, stepped to one side, put his other arm around his waist, an' did that hip-toss judo thing we'd learned last summer from the *Judo Joe* comic book I had when Frances Ann came to visit.

Billy rolled over Hutch an' landed flat on his back, right on top of several of our metal toy cars. That had to hurt, too.

"Ow, ow, ow." He rolled back over an' grabbed his back.

That Jimmy Jack fella I'd hit, put both hands to his face, then pulled 'em back an' looked at the blood all over 'em.

His eyes got all big an' mean lookin' as he glared up at me.

Tiny ran up to him with her rar-rar-rar bark an' growl like she does, an' started chewin' an' shakin' on one of his arms. He slung her away, causin' her to tumble all the way over to one of the sycamore trees out front. She yelped real loud when he did.

Then he jumped to his feet an' charged at me. "Damn you...little punk!" He grabbed the front of my jacket again an' commenced to slappin' me back an' forth across my face—bustin' my lip.

Hutch ran at him, head-buttin' his hip—without much effect. Jimmy Jack backhanded him, knockin' him arollin' just like Tiny, but in the other direction. Then he drew back his fist...

§§§

CHAPTER SIXTEEN

WORTHAM'S FEED

Sheriff Wilson, John, and Joe walked over to the group of men standing off to the side of the store.

The sheriff nodded at the three men. "Mace, Ed, J.W., ya'll see anybody else here?"

Mace looked at Ed and then back to the sheriff. "Stopped when we saw Pete an' Charlie pull in...was right behind J.W. Thought Clive might be sick or somethin'."

"Little worse than that I'm afraid, Mace...He's dead."

Ed's eyes went wide. "Dead? What in hell? We seen him just this afternoon...late. Seemed fine to us." He and Mace exchanged looks again.

"Yeah, I was here almost to closin' time." J.W. Glanced at John and Joe. "When Big John an' that other feller there was here gittin' feed." He nodded at Joe. "An' what I took was John's grandson with a colored friend...What happened? He have a heart attack?"

"Not hardly, somebody beat him to death...At least three men."

"Lord, Lord...Robbery?"

"Rather not say at this time, Mace...You see anything or anybody around before you left?"

"No, sir, was on the way back from pickin' up some bologna at Smeads for

Myrtis to fry up for supper when I saw the ambulance pull in."

"Who was that fella sittin' eatin' peanuts with ya'll when me an' my son-in-law were in gettin' feed?"

J.W. looked over at John, then at Mace and Ed. "Believe he said his name was Albion Wheeler...went by Al. Can't say as I blame 'im."

"Hadn't seen him 'round here 'fore," added Mace.

The sheriff nodded. "Figures...All right, that's all boys. If you think of anything else get in touch with me at the office or go by John's and tell him."

"Sure thing, Sheriff."

The three men turned to their trucks, got, in and drove away.

Sheriff Wilson pulled out his little notebook from his shirt pocket and flipped it open. "Let's run by the box numbers over on Salem Road those two good ol' boys ya'll had that set-to with at the Iddledo gave me for their addresses..."

UNION COUNTY

"Dollar to a plugged nickel there's no such places, Myron."

"No bet, John, no bet."

JAMISON HOME

The whole front yard rang with a huge explosion that hurt my ears at the same time this big geyser of sand an' dirt flew up past my head from down by that Jimmy Jack's foot.

His fist, as well as everthing else about him, just seemed to freeze right where they were, except for him lookin' down at the crater in the dirt beside his boot. I couldn't see but I could hear, after my ears stopped ringin', grandma from behind me on the porch.

"Hit that boy again, you piece of trash, and you're dead right where you stand. I got another shell in this shotgun and I can take your head off without coming close to my grandson...Your choice."

"That goes for you, too, numbnuts." I could hear mama rack a bullet in daddy's bolt-action seventeen shot .22 he always brought with him to go squirrel huntin'.

Jimmy Jack let go of my coat an' I looked around to see mama an' grandma standin' side-by-side, like in a western movie, pointin' that shotgun an' rifle at Jimmy Jack, an' Billy, who was still layin' on our cars an' trucks.

Hutch was crumpled at the base of one of the trees like a rag doll, I turned an' ran over to him. He was out cold, the side of his face was swellin', an' one eye was swole shut.

I slid to the dirt beside him an' gathered him up in my arms. "Hutch, Hutch! Wake up, please wake up!"

"Is he all right, Foot?"

I looked up back at the porch. "No, Mama, he ain't...but he's breathin'. That Jimmy Jack there whacked him a good one."

I turned my head a little to where Tiny had been layin' an' Laddie was over there lickin' on her. I could hear her whine some as she sat up an' looked around. Guess she had her bell rung, too.

Grandma waved the shotgun at Jimmy Jack. "You...Lay down on the ground beside your friend. Don't either of you move till I tell you different...I'll only say it once."

"Yes, Ma'am." He dropped to the ground like he'd been poleaxed.

Grandma leaned the shotgun against the porch post just to the side of mama. "I'm going to go check on Hutch, Vertis. Don't hesitate to shoot either or both of these miscreants, if they move."

"The thought of hesitating never crossed my mind, Mama...and I think you're being too kind."

"John and them will be back shortly. They can deal with these two..." She glared at Jimmy Jack. "If they're still alive."

She walked on past them to where I was with Hutch.

Jimmy Jack an' that Billy character just stared at one another there on the ground.

There was a little dab of snow left at the bottom of that big tree on one side. She got a handful an' held it against Hutch's cheek, an' then rubbed her hand with a little over his forehead.

Hutch's eyes kinda fluttered then opened an' looked up at grandma.

"Am I dead?...Are you an angel?"

Then his eyes started blinkin' like he was tryin' to clear 'em up an' he finally was able to focus on grandma.

"No, not yet, Hutch. Not yet."

"Grandma Jamison!" His eyes looked around kinda wild-like, then he raised his hand to his eye. "Ow...What happened?"

I held his other hand. "You didn't duck, dummy."

"Oh, yeah, right. Didn't even see it comin'."

Grandma looked into his eyes. "Are you all right, Hutch?"

He blinked a couple more times. "Yessum, think so. Only see one of you, now." He tried to peer over at Jimmy Jack an' Billy. "Did I hurt either of 'em."

I smiled an' pushed his shoulder. "Not as much as they did you."

"Dang! Figured the one I threw over my hip would be a little banged up."

I looked over at Billy, still tryin' to rub his back. "Maybe did him a little. Hope he didn't break any of our toys."

Hutch tried to laugh. "He did fall smack dab on 'em, didn't he?"

"He did."

I looked over my shoulder as the sheriff pulled up an' stopped out front. Him, daddy, an' grandpa got out an' came into the yard.

The sheriff took everthing in at a glance, includin' mama still holdin' daddy's rifle on them two.

"Well, looky here, looky here."

He squatted down right in front of Jimmy Jack an' Billy. "Go looking for you boys at those bogus box numbers you gave me an' lo an' behold you drop right here in my lap. What do you know about that?"

Jimmy Jack an' Billy looked at each other.

"Think we messed up, Billy."

The sheriff grinned at Jimmy Jack. "You think?"

Daddy had his arms folded across his chest after he took in my fat lip an' Hutch's swole-up face. "Got a sayin' back in Texas, 'Believe you two crapped and fell back in it." He looked over his shoulder at me. "Ain't that right, Foot?"

"Yessir...Also heard that 'if the world were perfect...it wouldn't be'."

The sheriff glanced at me. "How's that again, Foot?"

I tried to smile but knew it looked funny with my upper lip. "Somethin' that Yogi Berra says, Sheriff."

"Ah, right. Yankee catcher. Think he also said, 'If you come to a fork in the road...take it'." He looked back at Jimmy

Jack an' Billy. "Ya'll should have done that."

Billy looked confused. "Huh?"

§§§

CHAPTER SEVENTEEN

JAMISON HOME

"Now, you boys want to tell me about what happened at Wortham's?"

Jimmy Jack and Billy sat handcuffed with their hands behind their back on the porch in front of Sheriff Wilson, grandpa, an' daddy. They looked at each other.

"Sir?"

UNION COUNTY

"Jimmy Jack, don't start by trying my patience. Not'n the mood...What happened at Wortham's?"

"We don't know what you're talkin' 'bout, Sheriff. We ain't never been to Wortham's."

Me an' Hutch had come back outside after mama an' grandma doctored us up. Wadn't much could be done, though. Tiny an' Laddie were with us. She wadn't none too steady, like Hutch, but she'll be all right.

They put some snow in a wash rag for Hutch's cheek an' eye an' just wiped the blood off my chin from my busted lip. It'd have to heal up on its own—wadn't the first one I ever had an' probably not the last. Got at least one fat lip a year playin' football. Maybe one of these days they'll have face masks for helmets.

We were payin' close attention to what was bein' said. Could tell daddy an' grandpa was wantin' to shake some answers outta them two on account of what they did to me an' Hutch, but the sheriff was doin' it his way—for now.

Billy glanced at Jimmy Jack an' nodded. "We don't got no idea what you're talkin' 'bout, Sheriff...Honest to God."

"Yeah, Sheriff...Did somethin' happen at that feed store?"

"You could say that, Jimmy Jack. Three fellas went in there this afternoon an' beat Clive Wortham to death."

Billy an' Jimmy Jack looked at each other an' both started talkin' at the same time, denyin' havin' anything to do with it.

The sheriff held up his hand. "All right, all right, hush-up...the both of you. Just hush." He looked at grandpa an' daddy.

"They may have a point, Myron. Look at their hands...an' the only marks on their faces is Jimmy Jack's busted nose he got from Foot."

We could see the sheriff's jaw muscles workin'.

"Well, much as I hate to admit it, guess there is something there, John. We know Clive put up a fight. His hands were all

194

bruised an' skint...did some damage to somebody."

"We didn't even mark these boys at that Iddledo fracas."

"Yeah, I noticed that, Joe."

"Does that mean we're off the hook, Sheriff?"

"Didn't say that, Jimmy Jack...Not counting what ya'll did to Foot an' Hutch, here. Got you on assault and battery for that...There's still the matters of the other string of murders that have been goin' on around here."

Hutch looked at me. "What's assault an' battery? They didn't have one."

The sheriff heard his question an' turned to Hutch. "Means they hit you boys with intent to hurt you."

Hutch touched the swole-up side of his face, an' then looked at my fat lip. "Oh! Yeah, they done that, awright."

The sheriff nodded. "That carries some jail time." He looked back at Jimmy Jack an' Billy. "Now, ya'll got that lookin' at you...Just remains to be seen if it gets worse."

Jimmy Jack shook his head. "We didn't have nothin' to do with them murders, Sheriff...Honest we didn't."

"Uh-huh, like you lived at those addresses you gave me...You were seen over by Miz Riggs place. Said yourselves you were on Ware Road, by the Ross place...Now, when were you on Salem Road?"

Jimmy Jack an' Billy looked at each other again.

Billy turned back to the sheriff. "What's on Salem Road?"

The sheriff got kind of a stink eye look. "Earnest Krause's house."

Both Billy an' Jimmy Jack paled some.

"Mean somethin' happened to old man Krause?"

"Could say so, Billy. He got killed, too...Now, when were you there?"

Could tell the sheriff was tryin' to trick 'em into admittin' they were there. Seen cops do that in a James Cagney movie last year.

"Uh, well, we done some fence row cleanin' for him last week...but that was the last time."

"Go in his house, Billy?" The sheriff looked a hole through him.

He looked at Jimmy Jack. "Well, we went in to get paid is all."

"Guess that was when you left your finger prints there?"

Billy's eyes got big. "Huh?"

"Or did you leave 'em there when you killed him?"

"No! No! We never touched 'im, Sheriff!...Did we, Billy?"

"Uh-uh...No way, no day." He glared at his friend. "Told you we shouldn't been lookin' at those gee-gaws on his bookcase, Jimmy Jack."

"We didn't keep none of em...did we?"

"Naw...'sides he come right back in the room with our money."

The sheriff looked at grandpa an' daddy, then back at them two. "Well, by your own admission, you were at all three murder scenes. Gonna hold you in my steel hotel till we get some more information."

"What are we bein' charged with, Sheriff?"

"Assault an' battery...for now, Jimmy Jack. We'll see about the rest...Help me get 'em up, John, an' we'll take 'em to my car."

Him an' grandpa got to their feet, hauled Billy an' Jimmy Jack to theirs, an' hustled 'em down the steps an' out the walk to his car.

They put 'em in the back. Guess he didn't want 'em ridin' up front with him.

He started up an' drove off towards El Dorado.

Grandpa watched him drive off, turned around, came back to the porch, an' sat back down in his rocker. He looked at daddy.

"What do you think, Joe?"

Daddy shook his head. "Don't know, John, I'm no expert, but I'd say there's some more folks out there. Now whether they're all in cahoots or not, remains to be seen."

"My thoughts exactly, Joe…You should be in law enforcement."

Daddy grinned. "Don't think so, John, rather do what I do."

"Well, you got a knack for this, too, though. Wouldn't be moving around all the time."

"Got a point." He got to his feet. "Going to go in and see if Mame has some coffee on…Coming?"

Grandpa got up, too. "Thought you'd never bring it up."

They turned an' went inside to head down to the kitchen.

Me an' Hutch glanced at each other. Maybe this is where I get my interest in solvin' crimes.

"Be right back."

I got up, ran inside, an' in less than a minute, came back out with my Big Chief tablet.

I sat back down, cross-legged, next to Hutch with my tablet opened an' took my pencil outta my overalls pocket.

"What are we doin'?"

"Gonna see if we can connect the dots."

Hutch frowned. "What dots?"

"Just an expression, dummy."

"You're the dummy."

"No, you already got that honor."

"How do you figure?"

I leaned toward him an' kinda squinted one eye, makin' fun of his. "Whose lips were movin' when you heard it?"

"Do what?"

"Just somethin' I thought up."

"Well, just unthink it."

"You can't unthink somethin'."

"Can too."

"Can not."

"Can too."

"How 'bout I give you one of these black eyes?"

"You an' what army?"

He held up both fists. "Mister right an' mister left."

I giggled.

"What's funny?"

"You tryin' to use mister right an' mister left with one eye."

He giggled. "Is funny, id'n it?...Now what dots?"

I started sketchin' on my pad. "The dots of the crime scenes an' that map I copied from behind old man Kruse's bookcase."

"Think you got somethin' figured out?"

"Maybe I do...an' maybe I don't."

"Well?"

§§§

CHAPTER EIGHTEEN

HAYNESVILLE ROAD

"Uh, Sheriff."

The sheriff looked up into the rearview mirror at Jimmy Jack and Billy in the back seat. "What, Billy?"

"I gotta pee...real bad."

"Can't you wait till we get to El Dorado?"

"No, sir. We stopped at the Iddledo an' had a pitcher of beer 'fore we went to the Jamisons an'...I gotta pee like a pet coon."

"He ain't no good at holdin' it, Sheriff, never has been. He'll pee his pants shore as the world...Not to say what'll go through to your seats."

The sheriff glared in the mirror at Jimmy Jack, then at Billy. "Well damn."

He pulled to the side of the road on the other side of the iron bridge across Three Creeks and stopped.

The sun was settling toward the tree tops to the left of the road to El Dorado.

Sheriff Wilson got out, slammed the door hard enough to break glass, stomped around in a tight circle twice, then opened the back door on the shoulder side.

"All right, get out...back there by the bridge an' do your business."

"Uh, Sheriff?"

"Now what?"

"Uh, can't."

"And why the hell not?"

Billy turned around showing his back. "Handcuffed."

The sheriff rolled his eyes. "Jesus, Mary, an' Joseph." He reached in his pocket got the key, unlocked one wrist and looked at Jimmy Jack. "If you need to go, too, better do it now. Ain't stoppin' again!"

Jimmy Jack turned around so the sheriff could reach his cuffs. He unlocked one wrist and re-locked the shackle to one of Billy's wrists—linking them together.

Billy looked at his and Jimmy Jack's arms cuffed together. "But how...?"

"You work it out. Ain't gonna draw you a picture."

Jimmy Jack looked at Billy. "Come on."

They walked back to the bridge where the iron frame sat on thick creosoted eight by eight pilings. Jimmy Jack gave some instructions to Billy that were out of the sheriff's hearing.

Jimmy Jack reached over to help undo Billy's pants with his free hand when the sheriff jerked around at the sound of a high-powered rifle from the woods on the east side of the bridge echoing through the creek bottom, followed quickly by a second shot...

JAMISON HOME

I looked at the map I'd drawn, and then sketched the locations of Miz Rigg's place on Sweet Road, Mister Ross' on Ware, an' Old man Kruse's on Salem on top of it.

Hutch leaned in an' studied the new map for a minute. "Wow, it fits...Ding dang."

"Yeah, an' look where it's goin'."

We both looked up when we heard the sound of two rifle shots comin' from the direction of Three Creeks. Me an' Hutch glanced at each other.

"That ain't right, Hutch."

"Uh-uh...deer season's over with."

We jumped up an' ran inside down to the dinin' room where grandma an' mama were settin' the table for supper—finally.

Daddy an' grandpa were already sittin' at their places working on cups of coffee.

"Daddy, Grandpa...just heard two rifle shots comin' from the direction of Three Creeks."

Grandpa looked at me. "What's that again, Foot?"

"Two rifle shots, right behind one another...*bang-bang*, like that...Sounded to me like it came from Three Creeks." I looked at Hutch. "Ain't that right?"

"I'd say so, uh-huh."

Daddy turned to grandpa at the head of the table. "We'd best go check it out. That's about where the sheriff would be...I'm guessing."

"Think you're right, Joe." He turned to grandma. "Best put our supper back in the warmin' oven, Mame. Eat when we get back."

"I know."

They got to their feet an' headed down the wide dog run to the front door where they grabbed their coats an' hats from the rack.

UNION COUNTY

"Can we go, Daddy?"

He looked at grandpa, then back at me. "Well, yeah okay, but you boys stay in the car…Understand me?"

"Yessir."

"Do you think that's a good idea, Bob?"

He looked back over his shoulder at mama. She an' grandma had followed us down the hall.

"Oh, I think so, Honey…Make 'em stay in the car. May not be anything at all, but just need to check."

Daddy went into their bedroom, had an idea he got his .45 from his suitcase. Sure enough, he had a bulge in his coat pocket when he came back out.

Grandpa went into his bedroom at the same time, probably to get the .45 automatic like daddy's he carried when he was deputyin'.

Tiny an' Laddie looked up at us.

"Ya'll stay here, be back in a bit." Could tell she wadn't all that fired up to go, anyway. Think she wanted to go back to sleep.

We went out an' got in daddy's Ford. He cranked it up an' we took off toward Three Creeks.

HAYNESVILLE ROAD

Daddy pulled past the sheriff's car on the other side of the Three Creeks bridge. The sun was almost completely gone behind the trees. It was what grandma always called the gloamin' time of day. Don't know why, looked like twilight to me.

The sheriff was crouched down on the road side of his car, had his gun in his hand an' was peerin' over his hood.

We could see the bodies of Jimmy Jack an' Billy piled on top of one another over by the bridge.

"Get down in the floorboard, boys."

When daddy used that tone of voice, wadn't no discussion. We jumped in the floorboard between the front seat an' the back. But I got where I could peak over the window sill.

UNION COUNTY

Daddy an' grandpa pulled their guns, both got out on the driver's side an' ran in a crouch back to the sheriff's car. They stopped beside him.

Daddy leaned his back against the side of the sheriff's county vehicle. I cranked the window down so's we could hear.

"What happed, Myron?"

"Ambush, John. From the east side. Swear to God it came from down the creek itself."

"Somebody in a boat just waitin' on ya'll to come by."

"But how the hell could they know?"

"Five'll get you ten Jimmy Jack and Billy were sent to your house, John. Told you I thought there were more involved."

"Could be right, Joe...Must have had it prearranged the boys would have to pee right before we got to the bridge if they got arrested...Billy acted like he couldn't hold it an' would ruin my seats, too."

"Yeah, bet they had it set up, all the way, Myron."

Daddy looked at grandpa, then the sheriff. "Got a feeling they were told it would be you that would be shot..."

"When all along they, whoever they are, were going to make sure it would be those two rednecks would keep quiet...permanently."

"Can't argue with that logic, John."

"What's it been since the shots were fired? Ten minutes or so?"

Could see the sheriff nod. "About that, Joe...Better call it in an' have Pete an' Charlie come out with the meat wagon...Getting too dark for anymore long range shootin' anyway."

Grandpa chuckled. "Told Mame to put the supper back in the warmer. Probably have to add another plate anyway for Doc Duckworth."

The sheriff shook his head. "Darn, I'd forgotten all about not ever sittin' down for supper. Mame's gonna have our hides. What'd she fix anyway?"

"Chicken an' dumplins...'spect she'll mix up a fresh batch of biscuits. Can't sop up the juice without biscuits."

"Oh, wow, God works his wonders in mysterious ways."

Could see daddy grin. "Smelled hot bread puddin' in the oven before we left."

"Oh, my."

He rose up, stepped to his door, opened it, an' sat down on the edge of his seat. We could hear him on his radio callin' his office. They would call the doc an' the ambulance.

Me an' Hutch looked at each other, think both our mouths were waterin'. We forgot 'bout eatin' too, what with gettin' the snot beat out of us, an' all the goin's on."

Figured it was all right to get up, so we did, an' sat on the seat so we could look out the back. Have to wait on the ambulance an' the doc to get there 'fore we could head back to the house.

Me an' Hutch decided to play rock, paper, scissors while we waited.

No one could see two men in a flat bottomed pirogue up the creek over a hundred yards. It was snugged up against the bank behind some brush hanging out into the creek just past a bend. They had a branch pulled down so they could see the bridge. The fading light was in front of them and two high-powered rifles with scopes lay on the seat in the middle.

§§§

CHAPTER NINETEEN

JAMISON HOME

"Anyone that doesn't like my dumplins, I'll make them a peanut butter sandwich."

We all knew grandma was funnin'. Folks all around seemed to know when she was makin' 'em an' would just show up, like the sheriff an' Doctor Duckworth—even the governor of

Arkansas, one time before I was born—mama said.

Grandma filled each plate with chicken n'dumplins from the big blue an' white tureen thing down at her end of the table an' passed 'em around the table. The tureen was too big to pass around.

Everbody helped themselves to the biscuits from two different platters.

The doctor took a big bite of a dumplin. "Mmm-mmm, Mame, you oughta patent these, they're just amazing."

"Oh, pshaw, Ralph Duckworth, you're just hungry."

"Well, that too, but even if I weren't, I'd still make room for 'em."

"Speaking of, better save room for my bread pudding."

He laughed. "Always, Mame, always. Been smelling it since we came in."

She looked at Sheriff Wilson. "Do ya'll have any idea who shot those boys?"

He shook his head an' dabbed his mouth with a napkin. "Not even a ghost of a clue. Just tells me there is a lot more to all this than meets the eye."

I looked at daddy, then at the sheriff. "Sheriff Wilson, I drew a sketch of that map thing you found at Mister Krause's an' I kinda laid it on top of where those killin's had all took place...'cept for Mister Wortham's."

He glanced at me as he dug back into his dumplins. "That's nice Foot."

"Might ought to take a look at it, Myron. Foot is the one that suggested to look behind that bookcase."

The sheriff hesitated in mid-chew an' looked at grandpa. He seemed to pause a couple of seconds, either that or he had to swallow.

"Could have a point there, John."

He looked at me. "We'll take a look at it after supper, Foot...Think it means something?"

"I don't know, sir, that's why I mentioned it. They seemed to fit right good.

"Well, Foot, right well."

I glanced at grandma. "Yessum, that too."

She grinned at me, shook her head, an' got up to go get the last batch of biscuits from the oven. Everbody likes grandma's biscuits almost as good, or maybe it's well, as the dumplins—not quite but almost.

"It doesn't make much sense, 'cause the map I drew leads to the middle of the woods between here an' Salem Road. Ain't nothin' there, is there, Hutch?" I glanced to him sittin' next to me.

"Uh-uh, not that I know 'bout...Been through there a time or two huntin' squirrels with my grandpa's single shot .22...Lots of hickory an' black walnut trees there...Purty thick."

"If it had anything to do with Bonnie and Clyde, would have been over sixteen years ago, wouldn't it John?"

"Yep, about that, Joe."

"What do you think those boys had to do with it, Sheriff?"

He turned to mama. "No idea on that, either, Vertis."

"We don't even know if they did the killings or not. My guess is they didn't...but they may have been there or been involved."

I looked up at daddy. "Maybe they were just scoutin' for somebody...ones who did the killin'."

The sheriff had his coffee cup halfway to his mouth an' put it back down. Had kind of a puzzled look on his face. He turned to grandpa.

"Well, well. From the mouths of babes."

Grandpa nodded. "It's the only thing that makes any sense, Myron." He looked at me. "Good job, again, Foot. May have to deputize you boys."

My eyes got real big. "Really?"

"No." The sheriff grinned. "But, might make you an' Hutch, honorary deputies, though."

I looked at Hutch, then back to him. "With a badge an' all?"

He almost choked on his coffee that he'd picked back up. "Well, we'll see...Don't go gettin' ahead of us."

I cut my eyes down. "No, sir." But I knew that he might just find a way to get us somethin' like that.

THREE CREEKS

The man in the bow stepped out and pulled the pirogue up onto the bank so his partner could also get out.

The second man picked up the high powered rifles as he moved forward. "Well, that takes care of two more loose ends."

"Yeah, those two couldn't have kept their mouths shut for ten minutes."

"Think the sheriff and the Jamisons know where it's at?"

"Could be. We'll keep our eyes on 'em, let them do our leg work for us."

"Good thought...cheaper, too."

"You think?"

"Let's go get a drink."

UNION COUNTY

"You buyin'?"

"Don't I always?"

They carried the pirogue up the incline to some thicker brush and set it down. After covering it enough to hide it from casual view, they walked on up to their vehicle, got in, and drove back to the highway.

JAMISON HOME

The sheriff leaned back in his chair near the fireplace. "All right, Foot, let's see your little map."

Me an' Hutch were sittin' in the floor 'cause the adults had all the chairs there were.

I opened my Big Chief tablet to the last page an' handed it to the sheriff.

He slipped on his readin' glasses an' studied the layout that showed the roads, mainly Sweet, Ware, an' Salem where the murders took place.

I drew the map thing the sheriff pulled out from behind the bookcase at Mister Krause's over the roads an' those other places.

He handed it to grandpa an' turned to me an' Hutch. "Well, you're right, boys. Ends in the middle of the woods all right." The sheriff looked at grandpa. "John?"

Grandpa rubbed his baldin' head an' thought a minute. "Yeah...and it really seems like there was a home place in there somewhere. Just can't recall right off whose it was...Burned down years ago."

"Let me see that, John."

He handed my tablet to grandma. She looked at it, then gave it to mama. "Vertis, didn't you an' your brother, Dorris, used to go over that way to gather pecans an' walnuts?"

Mama glanced at it an' nodded. "We did. There was an' old house there surrounded by pecan an' walnut trees just like Hutch said."

"There wadn't no house there when I hunted that way. The trees were but the rest was growed up...You know, briars an' such."

She handed the tablet back to grandpa. "Well, that line from Krause's sure enough ends up there."

He looked at Sheriff Wilson. "There's something there, I'm thinkin', Myron."

"Need to go there and take a look then, tomorrow."

Daddy turned in his chair to the sheriff. "Uh, one problem, Sheriff. I'm convinced we're being watched." He scratched the evenin' stubble on his chin. "How about we let the boys go through the woods to Dud's, get Tom Rayford, and they all go from there to check out that area of pecan and walnut trees on foot...Betcha that's the old home place you mentioned."

"We can do that, Daddy." I looked at Hutch. "Can't we, pard?"

"Uh-huh. Love seein' Mister Tom. He's the only Marine Corps Medal of Honor person I know...Fact is, the only Medal of Honor person I know of, period."

"Yeah, me too."

"Ya'll fill him in with every detail you can remember, hear?"

We both looked at the sheriff an' nodded.

"He'll know what to do an' what to watch out for. Tom's one of a kind."

I grinned big. "Yessir, Mister Tom is that."

§§§

CHAPTER TWENTY

JAMISON HOME

After breakfast, me an' Hutch grabbed our canteens, he picked up his grandpa's single shot .22 he'd brought from home, an' daddy handed me his seventeen shot bolt action .22.

"Now you boys know not to chamber these till you're going to shoot, don't you?"

I nodded. "We know, Daddy. Just makin' it look like we're goin' squirrel huntin'."

"Right...We'll watch an' make sure nobody's followin' ya'll down into the pasture. We'll be able to see you till you hit the woods at your grand daddy's fence line. Be sure not to crawl through holding 'em, now."

"Yessir." He said that evertime I went huntin'.

"Nobody around here knows how to get to Dud's anyway."

We looked at grandpa. "No sir...not even to his pond...'cept us."

"You boys be careful, now, you hear?"

I nodded. "We will, Grandma."

Mama an' grandma hugged us both.

I grinned at 'em "We'll be awright...ain't that right, Hutch?"

"Uh-huh, ain't nobody can follow me an' Foot in the woods...less we want 'em to."

I bumped his shoulder. "That's a fact."

UNION COUNTY

Grandma handed us each a brown paper sack. "Here's some ham sandwiches, in case ya'll get hungry an' Dud or Tom don't have anything to fix...I also wrapped up some fresh butter for them in your sack, Foot. Know they have to be about out."

We both grinned.

"Yessum."

I knelt down in front of Tiny. Little Laddie sat right beside her.

"You better stay here with Laddie, Tiny. He's too little to go, he'd tire out before we got halfway there." She cocked her head as she listened to me—know she knew what I was sayin' cause of the little whine she let out. "We'll be back later."

Everbody followed us out on the porch to watch us walk down through grandpa's pasture to the woods.

"Wonder where they're goin'?" A man watched as they walked to the gate next to the barn.

His partner took the field glasses he handed to him and watched the boys head off through the pasture.

"Goin' huntin', I'd say. Got their .22s with them. We need to keep our eyes on the big man and his son-in-law. If they know where it is, they're going to go to it sooner or later."

"Maybe so."

"Count on it. Won't be able to keep away...Especially if the sheriff comes back out."

DUD'S WOODS

We worked our way through the woods toward Unka Dud's pond.

The gray an' fox squirrels fussed at us 'cause they were scavengin' for any hickory nuts or pecans they might have missed earlier in the fall.

"We'll have to shoot some squirrels on the way back just to show we know how to hunt."

"Yeah, good idea."

The cardinals were flittin' about lookin' for seeds too. The red ones were the males an' brown ones were the females. Always thought that was strange but grandpa told me the females are harder to see that way. Guess it's mother nature's way of protectin' 'em when they're nestin'.

Didn't take long till we got to Unka Dud's pond. It was still black an' spooky as ever. Bet it didn't even freeze over durin' the cold snap deep in these woods like it is, plus the fact that it's spring fed. Unka Dud says it stays pretty much the same temperature year 'round.

We only got about halfway 'round the pond when Mister Tom stepped out of the woods in front of us. Scared Hutch an' me both, half to death—never heard him comin'.

He was stayin' over here 'cause Unka Dud had got shot by those German Nazi guys that were here last year from Argentina lookin' for him an' the treasure they thought he took from Germany before that first World War.

Him an' Unka Dud killed 'em all, though. Me, Hutch, an' my cousin Fran from Texas that was visitin', helped. We pestered 'em a bunch an' got 'em lost so they couldn't find Unka Dud's cabin.

"Hey, boys, what brings you over this way?"

"Oh, wow, hey, Mister Tom, grandpa sent us to get you to help us do somethin'...Grandma sent ya'll some fresh butter, too."

"Have to thank her...Well, ya'll come on to the house, we'll talk about it."

We continued the way we had been walking and went back into the woods on the other side of the lake. It didn't take long as it was only about a hundred yards to the pretty well hidden house.

It was a log cabin built into the side of a hill. There was two hidden chambers, one back underneath the hill an' the other underneath that one. One was his cool room for keepin' vegetables, milk, butter, an' stuff. The other underneath was where Unka Dud had hidden the religious treasures the Nazis were after.

Hutch, me, Mister Tom, grandpa, daddy, Sheriff Wilson, an' Fran, were the only other people in the world that knew about it.

Unka Dud was gettin' pretty well healed up from his gunshot, but Mister Tom was still stayin' with him for a while longer, takin' care of him—choppin firewood an' the like. Grandpa brought whatever supplies they needed from time to time.

Mister Tom opened the door. Unka Dud was sittin' in his chair near the fireplace readin'. Think he likes to read more'n me. Had a real library along one wall. His orange tabby, Gauner, was laying in his lap, sleepin'.

"Well, hello, boys, nice to zee you...Foot. Joe take hiz vacation early?"

"Yessir, wanted to get away from the snow up in Colorado, Sheriff Wilson thought we musta brought it with us."

He chuckled. "Might have ze point zhere."

"Grandma sent some fresh butter."

I reached in my sack an' took out the wax paper wrapped bowl an' handed it to Mister Tom.

"I'll put this in the cold room. Be right back." He opened the hidden door in the bookcase, went inside an' then came right back out.

"Now, the boys tell me John sent 'em about some kind of problem."

"Yessir."

Unka Dud pointed at the bearskin rug in front of the fireplace. "Have ze zeat, tell us all about it."

About thirty minutes later, me an' Hutch had filled in pretty much the whole story to Mister Tom an' Unka Dud.

"I remember zhat place. Belonged to Earnest Krause's zister and her husband, Ada Mae and Ofie Aguillard. Believe he vas related to zome Methvins in

Louisiana...Burned down fifteen years or so ago, faulty chimney. Krause's zister and husband died in ze fire."

"Grandpa, daddy, an' Sheriff Wilson want us to check it out with Mister Tom. They think the house is bein' watched by whoever's been doin' the killin's. Figured it would look like me an' Hutch was just goin' huntin'."

Hutch nodded. "Never follow us through the woods anyhow."

Mister Tom grinned. "You boys are almost as quiet in the woods as I am...make good Marines one day."

Me an' Hutch nudged each other.

Mister Tom looked at us. "Well, boys, shall we?" He got to his feet.

We glanced at Unka Dud an' he shook his head.

"Bit too far ze hike for me yet. But I'll hold ze fort down." He smiled.

"We'll leave our sandwiches for when we get back. Brought enough for you an' Mister Tom, too. Grandma made ham an' rat cheese on her fresh bread...some kinda good."

Unka Dud's eyes lit up. "Had Miz Mame's ham before. Iz goot."

I set the sacks on the counter an' Mister Tom led me an' Hutch out the front door. We turned to the left an' headed through the woods. Hutch knew how to get there, but Mister Tom did too. They said it was 'bout a mile or so—which through the woods would be 'bout a mile an' a half or better.

Took us around forty-five minutes till we came to the grove of pecan an' walnut trees.

We looked close an' could just make out where the house had been. There was a old stone well, mostly caved in, 'bout fifty feet over in some dewberry vines. We could make out what musta been the rock foundation piers for the house.

"Let's spread out boys, see what else we can find...lean your guns against one of those big trees, don't need to be carryin' them around."

"Yessir, Mister Tom."

We did what he said, an' then started pokin' through the brush round those piles of rock where the house had stood.

I stubbed the toe of my boot on somethin' stickin' up out of the ground 'bout four or five inches. Looked down at it an' tried to lift up—didn't move.

"Mister Tom what's this?" I pointed down at the iron ring I had tried to pull outta the ground.

He walked over, looked at it an' started brushin' the dirt an' stuff away from it. "Well, well, what do you know?"

"What is it, Mister Tom?"

§§§

CHAPTER TWENTY-ONE

JAMISON HOME

Joe looked over at John as they sat out on the porch having a cup of coffee in the warm sunshine. "Think the boys are there yet?"

John looked off across his pasture. "I would imagine." He turned to Joe. "What say we get in your car and drive over to

Krause's. Go inside like we're taking another look-see?"

Joe nodded. "Ah...like what they call a *red herring* in the mystery books."

"Close enough."

"Let's get it done."

They got to their feet, went inside and down to the kitchen to put their cups in the sink.

"Babe, we're going to make a red herring trip over to Krause's in case we're still being watched."

Vertis looked up from where she was at the counter chopping potatoes for a buttered potato and cheese casserole she and her mother were fixing as part of supper.

"Red herring?"

"Like mystery books...a phony trail."

Mame looked at them. "Oh, of course. Be gone long, John?"

"No, Hon, want to get back before the boys do."

"All right."

Joe and John grabbed their hats and light jackets and headed out to the car. They turned off Haynesville Road onto Salem, drove the short distance to Earnest Krause's house, and parked.

HAYNESVILLE ROAD

"What do you think they're doin' back there." He pulled the glasses down and turned to his partner.

"Your guess is as good as mine. We sure didn't find anything, but then again, we were in a bit of a hurry to get out of there."

"Point. Good thing we decided to keep an eye on 'em."

WOODS NEAR DUD'S

Mister Tom bent over with his hands on his knees lookin' at the iron top. "I do believe we have a trap door, boys. It's a fruit cellar or storm cellar...or both. Ideal place if they wanted to hide something."

I grinned. "Like Unka Dud's two rooms underground."

"Exactly."

Hutch had walked up from where he was lookin'. "We goin' down?"

"Yeah...but not now. Need to go back and get some lights. No tellin' what's down there. Good place for snakes to den up in the winter...if they can find a way in."

Me an' Hutch looked at each other.

He nodded. "Uh-huh. Hate snakes...ain't particular scared of 'em, but hate 'em. 'Specially in dark places like that...Can't see what you're steppin' on."

I grinned. "I stepped on one at Three Creeks when I was eight, was near dark...musta jumped five feet in the air, then ran like my hair was on fire."

Mister Tom glanced around. "Yep, they can do that to you...Let's cover this back up with leaves an' brush." He looked up in the trees. "Might want to see if ya'll can bag a squirrel or two while we're here...Plenty around. Need to take some fruits of your labor back with you."

Hutch frowned looked at me, then back at Mister Tom. "Fruits? Oh, you mean squirrels?"

He grinned an' nodded.

We grabbed our rifles from where we'd propped 'em. Got our bullets out of our pockets an' loaded 'em. Course Hutch's only held the one at the time, but I could put seventeen long rifle shells in mine.

"There's a lot of 'em around here because of these nut trees. Why don't ya'll sit down with your backs against those trees there." He pointed to two large walnut trees side by side. "Facin' in different directions..."

I nodded. "Uh-huh...They'll settle down an' get used to us an' go back to lookin' for nuts...You gonna shoot'ny."

"That's right. Let 'em come to you...I'll sit by that one over there. No, don't think it would be a good idea to use my Luger...It's a lot louder than ya'll's .22s...scare them back into their nests."

UNION COUNTY

Mister Tom had done lots more huntin' than us...not countin' durin' that World War I.

We plopped down against our trees an' got still. Sure enough, it wadn't no time atall till the furry little critters started comin' out of their nests an' holes in the trees an' went back to huntin' on their own.

Me an' Hutch knew to give 'em a little time to get settled in before we started poppin' a few.

Thirty minutes later, I had four an' Hutch had gotten three. Two of mine were fox squirrels an' one of his was—the rest were grays. They were a little smaller but ate just fine. Grandma will probably make squirrel an' dumplins, if she don't fry 'em up. Depends on what time we get back. Fried squirrel is near 'bout good as squirrel an' dumplins—tastier'n chicken, too, I think.

Daddy said that when he was a boy back in Texas, they called squirrel an' dumplin's, squirrel stew. But that a rose is a rose by any other name—whatever that means.

We picked 'em up an' tied their back legs together so we could sling 'em over our shoulders when we walked an' headed back to Unka Dud's to get lanterns.

Unka Dud looked up from his book he was readin'. It was *Land of Terror* by Edgar Rice Burroughs, my favorite author, book number six of the *Pellucidar* series. That's the stories he wrote about the world inside this one.

Haven't read that one yet—maybe I can borrow it from him before we have to go back to Colorado.

"Find anything?"

His cat, Gauner, didn't do no more than look up briefly when we came in, then laid his head back down on Unka Dud's leg an' went right back to sleep.

Mister Tom nodded. "Found what appears to be their fruit or storm cellar next to where the house must have stood. Going to take some lamps, go back and take a look. May be something...maybe not. We'll find out."

"Vhy don't ve have zhose sandwiches ze boys brought before you go back?"

He glanced at me an' Hutch. Guess our eyes lit up some. We both nodded.

So did Mister Tom. "Sounds good."

We sat down at Unka Dud's kitchen table while Mister Tom got the sacks.

"You boys want some buttermilk? Got some left from when John brought a gallon."

We nodded again.

"Uh-huh."

He went into the cold room an' came back out with a gallon jug little over half full. "I like it too." He put it on the table with three pint Mason jars for us to drink from.

"Vater for me, Tom."

He poured a glassful with the white porcelain dipper hangin' on the side of the water bucket an' set it in front of Unka Dud. Then sat down, opened the sacks, an' started passin' 'round the sandwiches.

Grandma always made 'em between two an' three inches thick—plenty of ham. There was rat cheese an' bread'n butter pickle slices with mayonnaise—no tomaters, though, this time of year.

When we finished, Mister Tom put our squirrels in the cold room, got three lanterns, we all carried one, an' we headed back out to that old home place.

Didn't take quite as long as the first time 'cause we didn't have to do any lookin' around.

Mister Tom lit each of our lanterns from a small box of matches he had in his pocket as we stood over the trap door. He handed his to me, bent over, after squarin' his feet under him, an' gruntin' a couple of times. That iron plate came up with a loud screech.

"Well, that hadn't been opened in a while." He held his light over the hole after proppin' the door back.

Smelled kinda musty like the air was real old. We could see some steps down into the blackness. Looked like they were made of local rocks an' cement—lots sturdier'n wood stairs woulda been.

He picked up a stick an' chunked it down in the hole.

"How's come you done that, Mister Tom?"

He looked at Hutch. "If they're any snakes, specially timber rattlers, they'll make a sound moving."

"What if it just makes 'em mad?"

He grinned. "Chance we'll just have to take."

Could see the whites of Hutch's eyes as they rolled up. "Oh, boy."

"Not to worry, I'll go first."

Hutch looked at him. "Yeah, but I heard snakes always bite the second..."

He looked at me. "...or third person to go by."

"I didn't hear any movement down there...Judging by the smell of the air, don't think any snakes could get in there." He bent over an' sniffed. "Besides, snakes always have an' oily smell...especially cottonmouths. They smell almost like a skunk."

Hutch's eyes brightened. "Yeah, they do, don't they?"

He got right behind Mister Tom as he ducked his head an' moved down the steps. I went behind him.

Mister Tom waited at the bottom till Hutch an' me got down. We held our lanterns high to light up the room.

"Gol-uh-olee!"

§§§

CHAPTER TWENTY-TWO

SALEM ROAD

"They been in there a while, must be really givin' it a going through." He handed the glasses to his partner.

"Yeah, let's see if they come out carrying anything. They must think they're on to something."

"If they are, we can count on them trying to go to it."

"And we'll be right behind them."

Joe peeked out the front window. "Think we're being watched, John?"

"Oh, believe we can count on it."

"Well, they can't know we found anything before." Joe paused for a moment. "What do you think about walking out with a folded over piece of paper...an' making a to-do over it?"

John nodded and grinned. "Now, that's an idea worth doing. They'll have to think we found something important...like directions or a map."

"Absolutely. See anything around we can fold over...sheet of paper or something?"

John opened a desk next to the bookcase, took out a sheet of writing paper and held it up. "Here we go. This'll work." He folded the paper one time. "Don't want to make it too small."

"Nope. Not if we want them to see it. Hold it up in front of me as we walk to the car. Maybe mouth, 'This is it', or something like that."

John looked at the folded to half piece of paper. "Yep, let's do it."

He stepped to the door, opened it and they walked out on the porch, then down the walk. John held the paper up shaking it slightly as they walked.

"We got it, Joe...We got it."

He folded it once more and stuck it in his jacket pocket before they got to the car.

"I think that was obvious enough, don't you?"

"Long as they were watchin'."

John grinned as he opened the passenger door. "I have no doubts. No doubts at all."

"They found something! They found something! Some kind of folded over piece of paper, I'd say." The first man put the field glasses down.

"Bet it's a map that shows Aunt Ada Mae's house...or where it was. Now to see what they do."

"Uh-huh...How come you don't know where your aunt's house was?"

"Because I was just a kid then. Never paid any attention. Just went along with mama an' daddy when they went to visit them one time...That's the only reason I knew her husband, a coon ass by the name of Ofie Aguillard, was kin to Henry Methvin someway who was a member of Bonnie an' Clyde's gang. They were goin' to Louisiana to visit his mama an' daddy in Bienville Parrish when they got killed by the cops."

OLD HOME PLACE

I reached over an' pushed Hutch's chin up to close his mouth. "If there were any flies, you'd be catchin' 'em."

"Would not."

"Would to."

"Would not."

"Would to."

"Okay, boys, enough...Let's see what we have."

The room which wadn't no bigger'n Unka Dud's cold room, was lined along the walls with wood shelves. Like most fruit cellars, there were the usual bunch of put-by Mason jars of peas, beans, tomaters, jams, pickled peaches, an' stuff.

But on two of the walls, the shelves were stacked with all kinds of guns an' boxes of ammunition. There were shotguns, pistols like daddy an' grandpa's .45, revolvers like the sheriff's .38, an' several of those machine guns you see in the gangster movies. They called 'em Tommy Guns, an' some kind of heavier rifle looking guns.

"What're those, Mister Tom?"

"Those are called BARs, Foot. Browning Automatic Rifles. We used them at the end of the war in Europe. They're bad news. Lot easier to get than a Thompson for gangsters, with more range and better accuracy...These have been cut down a little."

"I saw those BAR guns in that newsreel that showed the police that were at the shootin' of Bonnie an' Clyde down in Louisiana."

"Yeah. This must have been one of the places they kept guns for when they needed them...along with ammo. Some of them have a little rust, but not bad. Most of 'em have a light coating of cosmiline. This room is well sealed from moisture."

Mister Tom looked at the stacks of money on several of the shelves. "Not to say anything about where they hid their ill-gotten loot."

Hutch looked at Mister Tom. "Does that mean stolen?"

"It does, Hutch. It certainly does."

I looked the shelves up an' down. "Sure is a lot of it."

UNION COUNTY

Mister Tom nodded. "Could be as much as a hundred thousand dollars down here."

"Gol-uh-olee. That's all the money in the world."

He chuckled. "Not quite, Hutch...but it is a sizable amount."

I looked up at him in the dim light. "What are we gonna do with all this stuff, Mister Tom?"

"We're going to leave it right here. Need to go tell your grand daddy an' the sheriff. The rest is up to them...Let's go up, close the trapdoor, cover it back up, an' head to the house."

We got to the house an' Unka Dud had fallen asleep in his chair. His open book was in his lap. He woke up with a start when we came in the door. That scared Gauner, he jumped down an' hissed at us.

"*Guter Gott, vas is das?*" Unka Dud blinked a couple of times. "Make enough noise to vake ze dead...Vhat did you find?"

251

Gauner got back up an' laid 'cross his legs again when he saw it was Mister Tom an' us.

We set our lanterns on the table. I got a dipper of water an' shared it with Hutch while Mister Tom did the tellin'.

"Well, zhat is not surprising. I knew zhat Ofie Aguillard was related somehow to ze Methvins in Louisiana, but didn't know zhey vere visited regularly by Bonnie and Clyde. Kept pretty much to zhemselves. Not very social...Of course neither am I."

Mister Tom stepped over to the bucket to get a dipper of water for himself. "I'll need to go with the boys to show John and the sheriff how to get to the Aguillard place without traipsing through a couple of miles of woods."

"*Ja.*"

"Is there a old loggin' road or somethin' close by there, Mister Tom?"

"There is, Foot. Might be a little grown up, but there's one, or was, that goes within twenty or thirty yards of that house place."

"Might ought to wait till tomorrow, Mister Tom. The sheriff ain't at the house an' grandpa just wanted us to see what we could find."

He nodded. "Right, good idea, Foot. I'll come over in the morning. I'm sure your grand daddy will call the sheriff and he'll come out."

"Uh-huh...'magine so."

Mister Tom got our squirrels out of the cold room, we said good bye to Unka Dud, an' headed out toward grandpa an' grandma's.

We had made that trip so many times, could almost do it blindfolded—well maybe not quite, but almost.

"Looks like those boys are coming back from huntin'."

"Have any luck?"

"Got a couple of stringers of squirrels." He pulled down the glasses and frowned.

"You know, that direction they're comin' from is real familiar...seems like Aunt Ada Mae's house was down an old loggin' road that way."

"You don't suppose those boys might have seen something in those woods?..."

"Not supposin' anything, just sayin' is all...Also remember mama an' daddy tellin' about Aunt Ada Mae an' Uncle Ofie dyin' in their house when it burnt down."

"Yeah, when I was a kid an' went huntin', we went all over. Bet a sawbuck they've come across some ruins in those woods."

His friend got a sardonic smile as he watched the boys walk across the pasture. "No bet...One way to find out."

"I see you, but how?"

"Come on, got an idea."

§§§

CHAPTER TWENTY-THREE

JAMISON PASTURE

"Look, here come Tiny an' Laddie. Musta been up by the barn watchin' for us...Come on, girl." I bent over held, my rifle against my side with my elbow, an' clapped my hands.

We squatted down an' waited on 'em to get to us. Tiny ran up first on account she was lots faster'n the pup.

"Hey, girl, miss me?" She danced around my legs as the little feller finally made it to us.

Laddie jumped up on Hutch an' he picked him up to hug him good.

We headed on toward the house which was on the other side of the barn an' grandpa's equipment shed, an' the sand road down to Unka J.B.'s. The shed was where grandpa kept his single bottom moldboard plow, middle-buster, an' stuff that he used with his black-nosed Tennessee mule, Ted.

Tiny suddenly stopped an' looked at the barn on our right. She started growlin' an' the hair on her back stood up.

"What is it, see somethin'?"

We walked over toward the back of the old board an' batt barn that had, at one time, been painted red. Knew it was too late in the year for snakes. Thought it might be a skunk or possum or the like.

UNION COUNTY

Two men rushed out at us. One of 'em reached down to grab at Tiny—the other went for Hutch. Heard him scream.

"Run, girl, gee-ver! Go to the house."

She knew gee-ver meant to go home, so she took off. It was a word I invented a couple years ago for 'go girl' to teach her to run. Wadn't no chance of him or anything else catchin' her, she could fly.

I looked back up just as they got to us an' saw the knuckles of a fist comin' at my face. Next thing I saw was stars, an' then everthing went black...

JAMISON HOME

"Wonder if the boys are back yet?"

John glanced at Joe as they stopped under the bare-limbed sycamore trees out front. "Should be."

They saw Tiny jump the fence into the yard running from the pasture.

"Then again, maybe not."

Joe and John got out and looked back toward the pasture beyond the barn.

"Don't see 'em...you, John?"

Tiny had jumped up on the porch, turned around and looked at them.

"She appears cowed, not like her if Foot is coming back."

"Yeah."

John started toward the gate beside the barn with his long strides. Joe was right behind him.

They stopped at the gate and peered down the hill toward the pond in the direction the boys would be coming from.

Joe held his hand over his eyes to shade them from the sun. "Don't see 'em."

"Me neither...Hello, what's that?" John pointed back at the corner of the barn.

"Uh-oh, that's my rifle...and Hutch's grand daddy's, too."

"Along with two stringers of squirrels."

John opened the gate for him and Joe. They walked in and stopped at the guns and squirrels—then exchanged glances.

"Don't like this, John, not one bit. This is why Tiny was cowed. Somebody got the boys."

"And little Laddie along with them."

"I think maybe our red herring worked a bit too good."

John squatted down and studied the ground around the rifles and game. "Tracks leadin' that way...Looks like two men." He pointed toward the stretch of woods on the other side of the barn and shed.

"What's on the other side?"

"Red Hill Road, then more woods, then a loggin' road."

"Maybe we can head 'em off." Joe took off at a jog toward the woods on the other side of Red Hill Road.

"Can't keep up with you, Joe."

He looked back over his shoulder. "If they haven't reached the loggin' road, I'll hold 'em up till you get there. I'm going to hurt somebody."

"Go, then. Right behind you."

"Take the car, meet me on the loggin' road. Keys are still in it...In the floorboard."

"Got it."

John headed back to the car while Joe sprinted down Red Hill Road, then cut to his left into the woods.

It was a lot easier in the winter because everything except the pine trees were naked. He found a game trail and headed toward the Haynesville Road, knowing there was a logging road between Red Hill Road and it.

LOGGING ROAD

I blinked my eyes a couple of times. It was dark where we were, not pitch black, but dark. There was a kind of curtain in one direction an' on the sides, an' metal doors in the other with somethin' over the windows. We were movin'.

UNION COUNTY

I could make out Hutch layin' in the floor next to me. That's when I realized we were tied up an' in some kinda truck.

There was a man with a bandana 'round his face wearin' khaki pants an' shirt squatted on a bench along the side an' holdin' a rope that was tied around Laddie's neck. He was lickin' Hutch's arm an' whinin'.

I don't know how long I was out cold an' my head hurt like the dickens—'specially my forehead. It kinda throbbed. Think that's where one of the men hit me.

It wasn't long before I noticed Hutch stirrin' an' tryin' to open his eyes, just as whatever we were in slowed down. Laddie tried to lick his face but the man holdin' the rope wouldn't let him.

Whatever we were in stopped an' the curtain on my left opened an' another man, also wearin' a bandana 'round his face an' wearin' khakis, came through.

"Well, well, the babies are awake." He squatted down on the bench next to the other man.

"What do ya'll want?"

"Oh, we just want to know where ya'll've been."

"Huntin's all."

He looked briefly at his friend.

"Ya'll come across any old houses or burnt out ruins? Rock foundations?"

My eyes kinda flicked to Hutch then back to the man. "Not so's I noticed."

"What about your little darkie friend here? He see anything?"

"If I didn't, he didn't."

"I think you're lyin' boy. I saw you cut a glance at the nigger."

"I was just seein' if he was awake yet. He's my best friend."

The first man looked down at us an' sneered. "You got a colored that's your best friend?" He shook his head. "I've heard it all, now."

He kicked Hutch. "You see anything, nigger?"

"Don't call him that, it ain't nice."

He laughed hard enough to snort, the other man just chuckled.

"Nice? You think I care what's nice?"

He raised his hand to slap me, but the other man stopped him.

"I got a better way." He took the rope that was around Laddie's neck from him. "Whose mutt is this?"

Hutch spoke for the first time. "You leave him alone! He's just a puppy, he ain't hurt nobody."

"So he's yours, huh?" He looked at his friend. "That makes it interestin', doesn't it?"

"I'd say so."

"Now, I'm not a patient fellow. I think ya'll've seen something in those woods and we want to know what it was and where. I'm only going to ask this once more...Did ya'll see any burnt out ruins or foundations out there?"

Me an' Hutch both shook our heads.

The man lifted the rope up until Laddie was completely off the floor. His little legs were kickin' an' his tongue was stickin' out as he struggled to breathe hangin' there in the air.

Hutch's eyes got big. "No! Please, no!" Tears started to roll down his face.

§§§

CHAPTER TWENTY-FOUR

LOGGING ROAD

Joe burst out of the woods just as John drove up in the car. He looked down the road, then at the ground and squatted on his haunches.

John got out and walked up to Joe. "See anything?"

He shook his head. "Just tire tracks. We missed 'em."

"Not much telling where they went, either. There's all sorts of side trails off these old roads...could be anywhere in these woods."

The muscles in Joe's jaw rippled as he ground his teeth and slowly nodded.

John put his hand on his shoulder. "Don't think there really anything to be overly worried about, Joe. We know what they want."

"What can the boys tell 'em?"

"Nothing that I know of...Maybe Foot can draw 'em a copy of the map, but I really believe they'll contact us."

"Mean like ransom?"

"Exactly...Need to go call the sheriff. He's part of all this."

"But the thing is, John, we got no idea if there's anything there or not, plus really where..."

"Maybe we do. Hutch said he'd seen some old ruins and a dollar to a donut they took Tom there...He knows. We need to call the sheriff, and then trek over to get Tom."

Joe nodded. "At least we'd be doing something."

"Yeah...Well, Smead's store first and soon's Myron can get out here...We'll head that way."

"What if the boys won't tell 'em where it is..."

LOGGING ROAD

"I'll tell! I'll tell! Please don't hurt him!"

The man lowered Laddie to the floorboards. "Better be good, kid, or I'll string this mutt up an' gut 'em like a goat."

Hutch looked at me.

I nodded at the two men. "We'll show you what we found...Then you'll let us an' the puppy go?"

The two men glanced at each other.

"Why shore, kid. Just take us there an' we'll let ya'll go awright." He looked at his friend. "Won't we?"

"Well of course. Said we would."

I may be just eleven, but I know when I'm bein' lied to. Just gotta buy some time. Know daddy an' grandpa will do somethin'. Sure as the world they've found our rifles an' those squirrels by now. I wouldn't want to be in front of daddy when he comes—won't be pretty.

"We don't think there's any roads there, it's deep in the woods...we'll have to walk most of the way."

Hutch was quick to agree as he reached for Laddie, but the man wouldn't let him hold the pup. "Yeah. Gotta go down Salem Road a piece past the Baptist Church, then through the woods the rest of the way."

"How far is it?"

Hutch shrugged. "No idea, sir. Mile...maybe two. A ways."

I looked over at him. "Yeah, not sure we can get there 'fore dark."

"Don't matter. We got flash lights." He nodded to the other man. "Let's go."

That man ducked back through the curtain. Then we heard the truck start up an' it jerked some when he put it in gear. The old road was fair rough an' we bounced around some.

I looked over at Hutch an' he'd quit cryin'. Us an' Laddie were awright—least for a while.

The road smoothed out an' I figured we were back on the Haynesville Road, headed to Salem Road. Sure enough, in a minute we turned. I fell over on Hutch, but didn't hurt him none. Then the road got rough an' I figured we were past the church an' they found an' old road to pull off on.

JOLLEY'S STORE

"Yeah, Myron, get out here soon as you can...Uh-huh. Mame baked an apple pie...That's right. Fill you in when you get to the house. Laterbye." He hung the receiver on the hook at the side of the phone.

John turned to Joe. "He's on the way." He looked over at his cousin. "You seen any strangers around in the last couple of weeks, Smead?"

He shook his head. "Not so's you'd notice, John. Just my suppliers an' the usual salesmen...you know, the Stanley Coffee boys, LeRoux Brother's Coffee, an' others...mostly passin' through."

"Well, keep your eyes open."

"Usually do...when I'm awake."

John frowned. "Don't give up your day job, Smead. Ten thousand clowns out of work an' you're trying to be one."

He grinned back as John and Joe left the store and got back in the car.

When they pulled into the front of the house. "He'll be here in another..." John looked at his watch. "....eleven minutes."

Joe cocked his head. "That's hauling some, John."

"Yep, gave him a code word. He'll know to put a hurry on."

"What?"

"You heard me say 'Mame baked an apple pie'."

"Uh, yeah...Did she?"

"Not that I know of, but with her, you never know." He grinned. "It's just a code we've used before because of the party line."

Joe nodded. "Ah, right...Mabel."

"Yep, better'n a newspaper or the radio."

"Best go inside an' check our weapons an' get some extra ammo."

"Expecting trouble?"

John looked at Joe as they went through the gate. "Aren't you?"

He nodded. "Hurt those boys an' they can check their souls to God, 'cause their asses are mine...whoever they are."

"You will share?"

"Of course."

WOODS SOUTH OF SALEM ROAD

We were blindfolded, then they opened some double doors behind us an' helped us to the ground.

"Can't show you the way if we can't see."

"We know, we'll take the blindfolds off when we're in the woods."

Oboy. We walked a little way an' they did as they said an' jerked the rags off our faces.

One man pointed. "Go that way till you know where you are."

The other one handed Laddie to Hutch. He still had the clothesline rope around his neck an' he held on to the other end 'bout four feet away.

"Now, you try to run, I jerk this rope an' break his neck...Understand?"

Hutch looked down at his pup an' nodded. "I won't."

"I know."

We knew which way to go on account of the sun was on our backs. That told me the road had to be back that way an' that grove of trees was this way. Didn't know how far, but we'd have to wing it.

From the shadows, had to be gettin' close to sundown.

"This way ain't it, Hutch?"

He nodded. "Uh-huh." He held tight to Laddie but wouldn't look at the man.

I tried to stay to the thickest part of the woods. Had an' idea where the trail was an' stayed close to it. Didn't much care that there was branches just over our heads that had to be in line with their faces.

A limb swooshed over head as I pushed it up a little an' I heard the man behind me cuss.

"Dammit, boy."

The one behind him with the rope tied to Laddie was even louder.

"Son-of-a-bitch."

"Better not be leadin' us on no wild goose chase, boy. I'll gut that mutt right here."

"We aren't...sir."

I remembered a gully right close an' headed to it. Had to crawl down the side, jump a little branch about two feet wide an' clamber up the other.

"Ya'll hunted this way?"

"Yessir."

He looked up through the trees. "Don't see any squirrels out."

"They're up ahead a ways. There's some pecan an' walnut trees...Bunch of 'em there. That's where what we found is."

"Better be."

We ran out of ground an' came to the grove. Sure enough there squirrels out an' about like before an' the first man spied what was left of the rock foundation.

"Look! This is it, Albin! I remember it."

They started lookin' around.

The one called Albin kicked some of the loose brush around. "Hey, found somethin'." He uncovered the door.

The first man led me an' Hutch over to a couple of pecan trees fair close together.

"Sit." He pointed at one tree for me to sit down against. "You, here." He indicated the other tree for Hutch.

We sat down with our backs against the trees an' he took some heavy twine he'd been carryin' an' commenced tyin' me to mine with my hands behind my back. The Albin one used the rest of the rope around Laddie's neck an' tied Hutch to his.

"Now, you'll stay put, hear."

The first man lifted the door after he moved all the leaves an' brush Mister Tom had put there. He pulled out his flashlight from his back pocket, turned it on an' went down the steps. Albin was right on his heels.

They both started laughin'.

"Jackpot, my friend. Yeehaw! Jackpot!"

"Hot damn!...Just like we heard. Now to take care of those two snot noses."

§§§

CHAPTER TWENTY-FIVE

JAMISON HOME

John and Joe sat on the porch, checking and reloading their weapons when Sheriff Wilson rolled up. He turned the single dome red light that was flashing on top of his car off and got out.

John looked at his watch. "Dang! Nine minutes. Had to be doin' near a hundred...Good thing you're the sheriff, you would've gotten a ticket."

He grinned. "Waved at the Highway Patrol boys as I blew past 'em. They waved back...What's up?"

"They got the boys."

"What?"

"Remember Hutch telling us about the grove of pecan and walnut trees and Mame saying there was a house there once?"

"Yeah?"

"Well, the boys headed out there to get Tom this morning to take a look see an' Joe and me decided since we figured we'd been watched..."

"Uh-huh."

"We thought we'd lay a false trail to make sure they didn't try to follow the boys with their show of huntin' and went over to Krause's like we were doing some more checkin'."

"Yeah, this is getting good."

"Acted like we found something and waved a piece of paper like it was a map or something when we came out…"

"And they got the boys for some kind of ransom."

Joe and John both nodded.

"Got 'em just the other side of the barn before we got back. Found their rifles and a mess of squirrels."

"And the boys gone?"

Joe pursed his lips and glanced at John. "Hutch's pup, too."

"Whoever it is thinks they can make them tell what they know…one way or another."

"That's the way we see it." John looked to Joe.

"Figured we'd go get Tom and see what they found."

The sheriff got to his feet from the chair he was in. "What the hell are we doing sitting here, then?" He looked at the sun to the west. "Figure we got two, two and a half hours before sunset."

Joe looked also. "That gives us time to get to Dud's and see Tom."

He and John got to their feet and put their weapons in their pockets.

Mame and Vertis had come out the door and were listening to the men. Their arms were crossed tightly over their chests as they watched with concern over the boys while John, Joe, and the sheriff headed toward the gate to the pasture.

HOUSE RUINS IN WOODS

The shadows were gettin' long an' the woods darker as old man sun settled behind the tree tops.

We could hear them two gigglin' while they were apparently gatherin' up as much of that stole money as they could carry.

I was workin' like a crazy person to get loose. The man that tied me up—guess he was the leader or somethin'—hadn't done no great shakes of a job with the knot, I didn't think. Suddenly I felt it come loose where it was tied behind the tree.

I undid the rest, it was easy. Got my jackknife outta my pocket. They hadn't even bothered to check, scrambled over to Hutch an' cut that rope in two that had him an' Laddie tied.

Could hear 'em down in that hole.

"Gonna have to make two, maybe three trips, Albin, to carry all this money outta here."

"Yeah. I want them Tommy guns, too. This'un here got a sling."

"Slip it over your shoulder, then, an' let's get up there. Take care of those kids before we tote a load out to the truck. I don't want any witnesses in case they recognized me."

"Sounds good." He pulled the slide back. "Mag's full an' this baby's chambered...Can't wait to shoot it."

"Need to clean that cosmolene off...make it jam."

"Yeah, I know."

"Lead off then."

UNION COUNTY

They turned an' headed up the steps. Both had their arms full of bundles of cash.

The first man glanced around. "Damnation, those kids are gone!"

"Must not have tied 'em very good."

"Don't matter. We're gettin' out of the country anyway."

"I'd say it does, boys. You aren't goin' anywhere. You're under arrest."

They looked up as Sheriff Wilson stepped out of the shadow of a thick walnut tree. He held his .38 Police Special in both hands, aimed at the two men.

"Son-of-a-bitch! Take him!"

Albin dropped the money, slipped the sling off his shoulder, pointed the .45 caliber Thompson to where the sheriff was standing.

But he wasn't there. The sheriff stepped behind the three foot diameter tree as Albin squeezed the trigger on the machine gun. The chatterin' roar was deafenin' as bullets sprayed the big walnut an' everthin' around it. Chunks of bark an' limbs were fallin' everwhere.

Then it jammed.

"Dammit!"

Daddy stepped out from a pecan tree in another direction from the sheriff when that man looked down at his gun to try to fix the jam.

He charged an' barreled into him like a freight train while the leader man was droppin' his load of money an' pullin' his pistol from where it was stuck in his belt.

Mister Tom an' grandpa walked out an' both fired at him just as he was gonna shoot daddy.

My daddy was on top of that Albin fella, poundin' the dog poo out of him with both fists—could tell he was some kind of mad.

The other man jerked several times like a puppet on strings as Mister Tom's Luger barked an' grandpa's .45 did too—three or four times each. He spun around an' crumpled to the ground. Besides one leg twitchin' for a couple of seconds an' his heel drummin' on the ground like a woodpecker, he didn't move anymore.

Then the woods got silent as a graveyard at midnight. Not a bird one was singin' an' all the other early evenin' sounds just quit. Could smell what I figured was gunpowder in the air from all the bullets that had just been fired. My ears were still ringin'.

Didn't know it was daddy that got me loose till later.

There was money scattered everwhere. Mister Tom stepped over an' put his hand on daddy's shoulder to get him to stop beatin' on that Albin fella. He was out cold as a wedge of cheese anyway.

Grandpa looked down at the leader man all shot up, blood was coverin' the ground around him. He pulled the bandana mask down from his face.

"Well, well, what do you know?"

Daddy got to his feet an' stood beside grandpa. "Who is it?"

"Fabien Fontenot."

"That coon ass coffee salesman with the chicory coffee?"

"Yep. Said he was with LeRoux Brother's Coffee out of Louisiana. Probably a fake company."

The sheriff looked at Albin. "Have to wait till this one wakes up to get much more information. But it's apparent they were using the coffee company as a cover to hunt for relatives of Bonnie and Clyde."

Me an' Hutch had come out of the woods where daddy had us hide case there was any shootin'. Guess he figured there would be.

Hutch took the rope off Laddie's neck. He just jumped around an' pranced like he'd just had a bath or somethin'—ran over sniffed of Albin, lifted his leg an' peed on him. Think he was mad at 'im for bein' choked. He's a smart pup.

Grandpa rubbed the back of his neck. "Well, it's apparent one...or both of these knuckle heads probably had some kind of connection with Bonnie an' Clyde...or that Methvin family down in Louisiana they were headed to see. My suspicion is that's how they knew to come up here, looking around."

He looked at Mister Tom. "Good thing Tom here told us what they found an' the boys would most likely have to tell..."

I pointed at that Albin fella. "That one there was gonna hang Laddie...an' then gut 'im. We didn't have any choice, Grandpa." I put my arm around Hutch's shoulders.

"I know ya'll didn't, Foot, and it's all right. Would have done the same thing. It was just stolen money. Not worth anybody or thing dyin' over."

Daddy looked around. "Speaking of, guess we'd better gather up this money. It's all ready getting scattered by the evening breeze...You boys want to get started?"

The sheriff looked at daddy then at that Albin. "Did you kill him, Joe?"

Daddy looked down at him. "Oh, don't think so, Myron. Thought about it, but decided to just bust him up some...after I got started."

Mister Tom chuckled. "Think you did a good job at that, Joe. Hate to see you when you're mad...but I'll take you in my foxhole anytime."

Daddy smiled at Mister Tom an' nodded his head. "I would be proud to serve with you."

Me an' Hutch started gatherin' up all the loose money.

I grabbed the first handful. "Bet I can pick up mor'n you."

"Can not."

"Can to."

"Can not."

"Can to."

Daddy an' them just laughed at us.

§§§§§

PREVIEW
Of
The Next Exciting Addition
To the
SILKE JUSTICE SERIES

DALIA MARRH

CHAPTER ONE

VALLES CALDERA

"I never knew the stars could look like that." *Dalia Marrh* walked backward leading her snow white filly, Wind Runner, looking up at the expansive Milky Way that splashed across the night sky.

Silke and Haven Justice, along with Bone and Loraine, *Anompoli Lawa*, and

DALIA MARRH

Texas Ranger Riley Boston also gazed skyward, happy to see the stars and be home as they walked toward the horses.

Bear Dog scooted ahead toward his buddies, the horses left on this side of the portal, sniffing the familiar scents of home as he ran.

Dalia Marrh was the tall, slim daughter of Anasazi Shaman, *Enah Mahah*, Gentle Sky. She made it through the portal into the third world from the fourth of the Anasazi and the evil Skinwalkers before it was closed by *Anompoli Lawa*.

She had never seen the stars, moon, or the sun in her twenty-eight years in the twilight of the fourth world—this was her first time in the third world.

The horses nickered at their approach. They had been without water and the grass in their picket area was nipped down to the dirt.

The strains of the William Tell Overture wafted around the group, seemingly coming from nowhere.

Wind Runner was the first to be startled, reared up, whinnied, and pawed the air. The other horses also reacted, bucking at the ends of their tethers and stomping their hooves at the strange sound.

Loraine turned. "Bone! That's your phone's ringtone."

"Yeah, dang, who knew? Hadn't heard it in so long almost forgot." He fished it out of his possibles pouch, swiped the screen with his thumb and looked at the caller ID.

"Bone...Hey, what's shaking, Stella?" He turned to the others. "Lord love a duck, the vortex is fluxin' again."

BONE RANCH - 2020

"Damn you, Bone, we haven't heard from you for two months."

The 5'2" blonde bombshell Inspector with the Gainesville, Texas, Police Department glanced at her best friend,

Police Forensics Technician, Peach Presley.

The pair were house and dog sitting for Bone and his godfather, Padrino, at their six hundred and forty acre ranch in Cooke County, Texas. Bone, along with Loraine, had been transported from 2018 Texas to 1898 through a time travel type of portal.

Stella and Peach were in the root cellar with shelves on three sides loaded with put-by vegetables in Mason jars, jams, and preserves, along with fresh dug potatoes, onions, and apples in bushel baskets. It was underneath the kitchen at the one hundred and twenty year old house on the Bone ranch that belonged to Sheriff Flynn's sister and her husband, Cletus and Mary Lou Wilson, in the late 1890s and into the next century until they both passed away during the Spanish Flu world pandemic in 1918.

Sheriff Flynn and his wife, Deputy US Marshal Fiona Miller Flynn were Bone's great grandparents.

The Wilsons had sheltered the stranded alien, Lucy, and adopted her as an abandoned child. Lucy deeded the ranch to Bone in 2013 for saving her from some evil oil men when she was rescued by her people.

Stella and Peach were standing next to the Neolithic twenty inch tall solid gold statue with a three pound ruby mounted in the center that had been found on the ranch. The statue had been determined to be of the Paracas culture from between 100 and 800 BCE in Peru—predating the Inca.

Anompoli Lawa had postulated that the 7,000 carat ruby absorbed electromagnetic energy from cosmic rays and could activate a vortex that would connect to the past and Bone's cell phone if he was in an equal area of strong electromagnetic energy—per Einstein's theory of Special Relativity about the past, present, and future existing side-by-side at the same time in quantum entanglement.

"Put it on speaker, girl friend," said Peach, the Georgia native. "Hey, hidey Bone, how ya'll are?"

Bone's voice came through the speaker, "Hey, Peach, how you be, girl?"

"Bright eyed an' bushy tailed...Aw you know, mud an' magnolias, Bone...mud an' magnolias...Loraine there with yuh?"

"Yeah, couldn't prise us apart with a crowbar."

"Hey, Peach...Stella."

"Hey, Loraine," they answered simultaneously.

"Padrino, too?" asked Stella.

"No, he's back in Gainesville at Faye's...but *Anompoli Lawa's* with us. We're in New Mexico, near Santa Fe," replied Bone.

Stella and Peach exchanged glances and puzzled expressions.

"Thank God Winchester's with you to keep ya'll out of trouble an' make sure ya'll act like you got some sense...Now, what in God's green earth are ya'll in New Mexico for, Honey?"

"You wouldn't believe me if I told you, Peach."

"Bone, we already know you're three gallons of crazy in a two gallon bucket...If we can buy us talkin' over a hundred an' twenty years with a cell phone, we can buy most anythin' ya'll can get involved in."

"Well, you asked for it...We've been chasin' Skinwalkers and went through another kind of portal to their dimension known as the Fourth World where the missing Anasazi also are."

Stella and Peach looked at each other again, then down at Bone's dog, a blond and white pit bull named Tyrin—he cocked his head.

Stella took a breath. "You're right, Bone...that's a bit hard to swallow. Kinda like tryin' to eat some of Peach's baked possum and sweet potatoes."

Peach tugged at Stella's sleeve. "What the Sam Hill's a Skinwalker?"

"Ya'll remember those Caddo shape shifters that could change into giant wolves when we got involved with the Blue Water Woman?"

"Uh...yeah," they said together.

"Kinda the same thing...Except the Skinwalkers are evil demons, and damn hard to kill."

Stella leaned over to the phone. "I'm assumin' since we're talkin', ya'll got the job done."

"Could say. We killed a bunch of them and managed to close the 'always' portal to their world...lost a good friend, though."

"Anybody we know?"

"No, it was *Dalia Marrh's* father, *Enah Mahah*...Means Gentle Sky."

"Uh, who's *Dalia Marrh*, Bone?"

"She's an Anasazi maiden that came back through the portal with us. Her name means Pretty Moon." Bone turned to a once again wide-eyed *Dalia Marrh*. "Say hello to our friends, Stella and Peach...Just talk at this little box thing in my hand."

Bone held the phone facing her.

Dalia looked at the others, especially *Anompoli Lawa,* who nodded. She stared closely at the device, before leaning over. "Hello...I am *Dalia Marrh.* I am very pleased to meet you...I think."

Stella and Peach smiled and raised their eyebrows.

Peach pulled Stella's hand with the phone closer. "I gotta say, sweetheart, that your name's pretter than a speckled horse in a daisy pasture...*Dalia Marrh*...Just love it to death an' back."

Dalia Marrh glanced at Loraine who smiled. "Means they like your name...Think it's very pretty."

Dalia leaned forward again. "Thank you."

"You're just welcome as buttermilk pie, Honey."

Static started to build in Bone's phone. "Looks like we're losing connection and breaking up, kids. Try again soon...Laterbye."

"Laterbye, ya'll. It..." Peach's voice cut off before she could finish.

DALIA MARRH

Dalia turned to *Anompoli Lawa*. "I don't understand."

He smiled. "Well, I won't say it's simple, child, but it's very similar to the portal we just came through back in the cave except it was smaller and we were only talking through it to the future and them us. The portals can do several things, including going back and forth in time, besides going to other dimensions."

She blinked her big brown eyes several times, paused, and then looked at the venerable Shaman and nodded. "I see."

Bone smiled and looked at Loraine. "Well, that was nice...Betcha they do what they did with *Te Ata* after Silke met her at her induction into the Hatchet Woman Clan...and do a bunch of research on the internet."

Anompoli Lawa nodded and looked at *Dalia Marrh*. "*Te Ata*...Chickasaw, meaning, Bearer of the Dawn...Also a beautiful name. She became a great storyteller and spokesperson for the Chickasaw."

Dalia pursed her perfectly formed lips and nodded. "It is a beautiful name."

"Well, folks, let's get those horses down to the water before they get really mad...Ranger, we'll take care of doing that and picketing them on some fresh graze if you'll gather some deadfall and blowdown for the fire. Don't know about ya'll but I could use some supper."

The Ranger nodded at Bone and headed into the woods.

An hour later, the horses had all been watered and picketed on fresh graze. Everyone sat around finishing their supper of beans and bacon with cups of hot coffee. They all seemed to be gazing up at the stars that looked like millions and millions of twinkling campfires.

Silke glanced at *Dalia*. "Lot different than just starin' at pitch black isn't it, Pretty Moon?"

She nodded. "It is, it is indeed."

DALIA MARRH

Haven took a sip of her coffee and turned to the Anasazi. "I've been wonderin' *Dalia*, how is it you speak so correctly, I mean you livin' in the other world an' all."

She smiled. "My father, *Enah Mahah*, brought a number of books...what he called your classics through. He taught me to read, write, and speak your language when I was young. I read them all, numerous times...Plutarch, Herodotus, Sophocles, Plato, Euripides, Homer, Shakespeare, and your Bible."

Anompoli Lawa shook his head in wonder. "He was one of the most brilliant men I've ever had the pleasure to meet and know...He was a great doctor, too."

"I have often wondered what it would be like to study medicine, go back and help my people."

Bone reached forward with his glove, grabbed the pot, and refilled his cup. "Could happen, *Dalia Marrh*, could happen."

Silke looked off in the dark back toward the cave. "Could be some time before you can go back though, *Dalia*. We would have to find either another 'always' portal or an open 'sometimes' one."

"Know what goes with those, don't you, Cuz?"

Silke paused a moment. "I do, Haven...I certainly do."

§§§

AUTHOR

Ken Farmer didn't write his first full novel until he was sixty-nine years of age. He often wonders what the hell took him so long. At age seventy-nine...he's currently working on novel number forty.

Ken spent thirty years raising cattle and quarter horses in Texas and forty-five years as a professional actor (after a stint in the Marine Corps). Those years gave him a background for storytelling...or as he has been known to say, "I've always been a bit of a bull---t artist, so writing novels kind of came naturally once it occurred to me I could put my stories down on paper."

Ken's writing style has been likened to a combination of Louis L'Amour and Terry C. Johnston with an occasional Hitchcockian twist...now that's a combination.

In addition to his love for writing fiction, he likes to teach acting, voice-over and writing workshops. His favorite expression is: "Just tell the damn story."

Writing has become Ken's second life: he has been a Marine, played collegiate football, been a Texas wildcatter, cattle and horse rancher, professional film and TV actor and director, and now...a novelist. Who knew?

Ken Farmer's dialogue flows like a beautiful western river...it's the gold standard...Carole Beers

OTHER NOVELS FROM
TIMBER CREEK PRESS

MILITARY ACTION/TECHNO
BLACK EAGLE FORCE: Eye of the Storm (Book #1)
by Buck Stienke and Ken Farmer
BLACK EAGLE FORCE: Sacred Mountain (Book #2) by Buck Stienke and Ken Farmer
RETURN of the STARFIGHTER (Book #3)
by Buck Stienke and Ken Farmer
BLACK EAGLE FORCE: BLOOD IVORY (Book #4)
by Buck Stienke and Ken Farmer with Doran Ingrham
BLACK EAGLE FORCE: FOURTH REICH (Book #5) by Buck Stienke and Ken Farmer
AURORA: INVASION (Book #6 in the BEF) by Ken Farmer & Buck Stienke
BLACK EAGLE FORCE: ISIS (Book #7) by Buck Stienke and Ken Farmer
BLOOD BROTHERS - Doran Ingrham, Buck Stienke and Ken Farmer
DARK SECRET - Doran Ingrham
NICARAGUAN HELL - Doran Ingrham
BLACKSTAR BOMBER by T.C. Miller
BLACKSTAR BAY by T.C. Miller

BLACKSTAR MOUNTAIN by T.C. Miller
BLACKSTAR ENIGMA by T.C. Miller

HISTORICAL FICTION WESTERN
THE NATIONS by Ken Farmer and Buck Stienke
HAUNTED FALLS by Ken Farmer and Buck Stienke
HELL HOLE by Ken Farmer
ACROSS the RED by Ken Farmer and Buck Stienke
BASS and the LADY by Ken Farmer and Buck Stienke
DEVIL'S CANYON by Buck Stienke
LADY LAW by Ken Farmer
BLUE WATER WOMAN by Ken Farmer
FLYNN by Ken Farmer
AURALI RED by Ken Farmer
COLDIRON by Ken Farmer
STEELDUST by Ken Farmer
BONE by Ken Farmer
BONE'S LAW by Ken Farmer
BONE & LORAINE by Ken Farmer
BONE'S GOLD by Ken Farmer
BONE'S ENIGMA by Ken Farmer
SILKE JUSTICE by Ken Farmer
SILKE'S QUEST by Ken Farmer
NO TIME to DIE by Buck Stienke

SILKE'S RIDE by Ken Farmer
ANGEL JUSTICE by Ken Farmer
SKINWALKER JUSTICE by Ken Farmer
DALIA MARRH by Ken Farmer

SY/FY
LEGEND of AURORA by Ken Farmer & Buck Stienke
AURORA: INVASION (Book #6 in the BEF) by Ken Farmer & Buck Stienke

HISTORICAL FICTION ROMANCE
THE TEMPLAR TRILOGY
MYSTERIOUS TEMPLAR by Adriana Girolami
THE CRIMSON AMULET by Adriana Girolami
TEMPLAR'S REDEMPTION by Adriana Girolami

MYSTERY
BONE'S PARADOX by Buck Stienke
RECIPE for MURDER by Ken Farmer & Buck Stienke
SIN NO MORE by Ken Farmer & Buck Stienke
THE LOCK BOX by Terry D. Heflin
THREE CREEKS by Ken Farmer
RED HILL ROAD by Ken Farmer
THE POND by Ken Farmer
UNION COUNTY by Ken Farmer

CIVIL WAR ESPIONAGE ROMANCE
SCARLET HEM by Terry D. Heflin
GOLDEN CIRCLE by Terry D. Heflin

CIVIL WAR ESPIONAGE ROMANCE
THE AMATHYST by Terry D. Heflin

HISTORICAL FICTION WESTERN
McGRATH by T.C. Miller

HISTORICAL FICTION ROMANCE
DAUGHTER of HADES by Adriana Girolami
ZAMINDAR and the LADY by Adriana Girolami

SY/FY
ANTAREAN DILEMMA by T.C. Miller

TIMBER CREEK PRESS